The camp grew quiet. For some reason, Jason wasn't sleepy. He was still reading when he heard another noise outside. It sounded like his bear visitor from the other night. He waited, marking its movements by the snapping of twigs. Like before, it snuffled at his tent and then kept going. Soon the camp was silent once again.

Five minutes later, Jason was about to click off his flashlight when he heard a high-pitched scream outside. It sounded like Tait or Brandon.

At first he thought the staff had sneaked back to scare them. Sleeping outside like that, they were easy targets. But this time, the shrieks didn't end in giggles.

"Help me! Please help me!" someone cried again.

Still half convinced it was a joke, Jason jumped up and slipped into his shoes. He kept his flashlight in hand.

"Jason, help me!" It was Tait.

On cover: The real Jason Francois from *Bear Attack*

"Author Deborah Morris is a wonderful storyteller, including conversations and events surrounding the actual adventure to let the reader get to know the kids involved."

—*A Closer Look*

"The stories are extremely well written and capture the excitement. The conversational style makes for quick reading."

—*Christian Retailing*

NUMBER 3

Bear Attack
Tornado
Blanco River Rescue

True Stories by
Deborah Morris

An Adventure Ink book / published by
arrangement with the author.
Printed in Canada

PRINTING HISTORY
This book was originally published in 1996 by Broadman & Holman Publishers as *Real Kids Real Adventures #6: Tornado.*
Published in 1997 by Berkley Books as *Real Kids Real Adventures #3: A Powerful Tornado.*

Dewey Decimal Classification: JSC
Subject Heading: Adventue and Adventures \
Lifesaving—Stories, Plots, etc.
ISBN 1-928591-04-3

Cover design by Doug Downey
Text design by Sheryl Mehary

Adventure Ink books are published by
BookPartners, Inc.
For information:

An imprint of ***BookPartners, Inc.***
P. O. Box 922
Wilsonville, Oregon 97070

To my "grand-dog," Puppet,
the only dog I know
who has her own subscription
to Reader's Digest

Bear Attack

The Jason Francois Story

Above: Jason Francois, age 16

"Good shot, Mountain Man! Someday you might even be as good as me."

Jason Francois, sixteen, lowered his rifle and kicked some of the powdery desert sand toward his fourteen-year-old friend, Jason Maddux. "Dream on. I can outshoot you anytime. And that's with my eyes closed!"

The teenagers were target shooting in the desert outside Douglas, Arizona. It was a peaceful spot, hilly and dotted with thorny catclaw bushes. So far they had "killed" a tin can, a cactus, and a broken mesquite branch. The desert animals wisely stayed out of sight.

The younger boy pointed his rifle at the sand. "I wish a rattlesnake would slither by so we could have a moving target. This is getting a little boring."

"Forget it, Ponga. You're not supposed to blow away rattlesnakes just for fun."

Jason Maddux had earned the odd nickname on one of their Boy Scout camping trips. Late one night, sitting up in their tent, they had decided to make up a secret language. Jason Maddux had come up with the word *ponga.* He wasn't sure what it meant, but he liked using it:

"It's a ponga night outside, isn't it?"

"Can I borrow your ponga?"

"Let's go ponga Bob's tent."

"I feel really ponga!"

From then on, he was "Ponga." In return, he dubbed Jason Francois "Mountain Man." Both of them were still Boy Scouts, but in different troops.

The "Mountain Man" nickname fit Jason. It wasn't that he was wild and hairy, though he had been trying to grow a mustache. So far all he had squeezed out were a few straggly hairs. But as a Life Scout, the second highest rank in Boy Scouts, he knew a lot about outdoor survival and tracking wild animals. On camping trips, he taught younger scouts about skunks, raccoons, and wildcats. Sometimes he even trapped animals so they could see them up close.

His favorite catch so far was a ringtail cat. He had set a trap near camp one night, hoping to catch a raccoon or jackrabbit. It was a "live trap," a wire cage with bait inside made to capture animals without hurting them. The next morning, hearing a loud scream from that direction, he found an angry ringtail cat inside, glaring at him through the wire.

He squatted down beside the trap, admiring the hissing, snarling animal. It was long and black, about the size of a fat skunk, with big white rings around its tail. He finally lifted the wire cage and carried it back to camp, careful to keep his face and hands out of reach.

The younger scouts were talking and eating breakfast. When Jason walked in with the cat, they all dropped their plates and ran over. He held it up, warning them to stay back.

"This is a ringtail cat," he explained. "They're an endangered species, so you won't often see one. If you ever do see one, don't mess with it. They can be dangerous." He nodded toward the cage where the cat was gnawing angrily at the wire. "They have sharp claws and teeth, and they like to eat critters like rats and squirrels. And Cub Scouts."

Laughing, the boys crowded around him. They begged to go along when he took the cat back out into the woods to release it, but he made them stay behind. He didn't want his joke about a scout-eating cat to come true!

Later, on that same trip, Jason trapped a ground squirrel and let it loose in one of the boys' tents while he was sleeping. The squirrel woke him up by scampering across his face. When the boy screamed, the frightened squirrel dashed for cover—down into his sleeping bag! That Cub Scout probably set a world record for shooting out of his sleeping bag and dashing from his tent. He was red-faced when Jason showed him it was only a friendly little squirrel.

The teenager's interest in wild animals had started back on his very first Boy Scout camping trip when he was thirteen. His first night out a skunk had waddled into camp and sprayed their troop dog, Shadrack. The poor dog was so miserable that they had to give him a bath in V-8 juice. Jason's hands ended up stained tomato-red, and for days a slight skunky smell hovered around him.

But that wasn't all. His second night in camp there was another unwelcome visitor—a black bear. The bear ambled up after they were in bed and started sniffing around for something to eat.

Luckily, the assistant scoutmaster had made them put all their food in the back of his truck, away from their tents. "In bear country," he had explained, "you don't store food or garbage in or near your tent unless you want to be Purina Bear Chow. If you don't have a car, you should put your food in a garbage sack and hang it from a high tree branch. Smaller animals won't be able to reach it, and it'll at least discourage bears." He laughed. "'Course, if a bear really wants something, he'll usually get it!"

That night, the black bear proved his point. It climbed into the back of the truck and dragged their coolers up the side of the mountain. After finishing off all their steaks and hot dogs, the bear gnawed the coolers for "dessert," leaving deep toothmarks in the plastic. Jason decided then to learn more about the wild things that roamed the woods.

Off to Polaris

Now three years later, he was looking forward to another big camping trip. That weekend he was going to a Polaris camp, where Boy Scouts from troops all over Arizona would meet for leadership training.

"I wish you were going to Polaris with us," Jason said as he and Jason Maddux started back toward the car. "It sounds like fun."

The other boy shrugged. "You have to be First Class or above, and I'm still a lowly Tenderfoot. How long will you be gone?"

"A week. It's at Camp Victorio, up in the Chiricahua Mountains." Jason grinned. "Maybe I'll catch a mountain lion and bring it back with me."

"Uh-huh. I can just see your mom if you walk in with a mountain lion. Before it could even roar, she'd have it tranquilized and snoring!"

Jason's mother, an anesthetic nurse at Copper Queen Hospital, worked all day putting people to sleep before operations. His father worked at a different hospital, managing the X-ray department. With both parents working at hospitals, Jason had picked up a lot of very important health tips. One of them was, "Never bring home mountain lions." If the lion didn't end up killing him, his mother would!

The Polaris camp would start that Saturday night. That afternoon, Jason stuffed a week's worth of clothes and camping gear into his backpack. He had gotten permission to drive himself to the camp, which was two hours away. His mother wasn't too happy about it, but that was the only way he could get there. As Jason packed, she kept warning him about his driving.

"There's a lot of loose gravel, so take the corners slow," she said. "Those mountain roads wind around a lot too. You haven't been driving all that long. Be careful!"

Jason grinned. "I'll try to keep my speed down to under a hundred miles per hour. Don't worry, Mom. I'll be fine."

Peggy Francois waved doubtfully as he pulled out of the driveway. Jason waved back, shaking his head at her worried expression. Since she worked in a hospital, she always imagined bad things were going to happen. But he was a good driver. He pointed the car toward the mountains and stomped the gas.

The drive passed quickly. Not *too* quickly; he went the speed limit at least most of the time. As he started up into the mountains, the narrow road grew steeper and more wooded. Even though it was June, the air was nice and cool. Jason rolled down his window and took a deep breath. He liked all the tree smells. Tree barks all smelled different, some sweet like butterscotch and others more sharp and spicy. If he ever lived in the woods long enough, he thought he could learn to identify trees just by their scents.

Finally, a small sign beside the road said Camp Victorio. He turned off and bumped his way along the dirt road until he reached the camp.

At first glance it looked like a small tent city had sprung up in the middle of the woods. There were dozens of tents, all different colors and shapes: dome tents, cabin tents, pop-up tents, pup tents. Boy Scouts of all ages were milling around like ants. Jason pulled into the small parking lot off to one side.

One of the scoutmasters spotted him. "Find someplace to pitch your tent!" he shouted. "We're camping here tonight!"

Jason nodded. Dragging his dome tent out of the car, he wandered around until he found an empty space under a tree. He put up his tent and threw his backpack inside.

Nothing big was planned for that night. The real action wouldn't start until the next day. Jason met some of his neighbors and then ate the sack dinner he had packed. At bedtime the familiar smells of tent canvas and mosquito repellent and the sounds of muffled laughter lulled him to sleep. Camping was great!

The next morning, a tortured bugle blast startled the camp awake at six o'clock. Jason jumped up, still zipped wormlike in his sleeping bag. Was it already morning? He scratched his head and then eagerly checked his mustache. He was almost sure it felt longer than it had the night before.

In Boy Scout camp, mornings started with a flag-raising ceremony. Jason fought his way out of his sleeping bag and stumbled outside, knocking over his lantern and backpack on the way. He left them lying there. He would be moving his tent that morning anyway.

After the flag ceremony, the scoutmaster announced that it was time to break up into patrols. To teach the boys to be leaders, he divided them into patrols of eight and gave each boy a turn as a leader. On the last day of camp, permanent patrol leaders would be chosen.

The scoutmaster had a list ready. "Okay, when you hear your name, come up here. Patrol number 1! You'll have…."

He read off eight names, all chosen from different parts of the state. After Patrol 7 moved off, Jason heard his name. He made his way to the front to meet the rest of his patrol.

The other boys looked relieved when he walked up. They were all much younger than he was, ranging in age from twelve to fourteen. Jason smiled. No matter who was assigned as patrol leader, he had a feeling he would end up having to help out a lot.

Patrol 8 to City Rats

One of the twelve-year-olds walked over. “Hi,” he said, sticking out his hand and grinning shyly. “My name’s Tait. I’m from Tucson. Where’re you from?”

“I’m from Douglas. My name’s Jason. Glad to meetcha.” Jason shook Tait’s hand and turned to the others. “So, who are all you guys? Since we’re spending the next week together, we might as well start getting to know each other.”

“I’m Brandon. I’m from Tucson too.”

“I’m BJ.”

“I’m John.”

“I’m Matt.”

One by one, they all introduced themselves. Jason decided they looked okay, even though they were young.

After the patrols were chosen, the scoutmaster called them to order. “Who’s ready for breakfast?” he shouted.

“Me!” roared all the boys.

“Good! Then I guess you’ll want to go find your campsites so you can cook it. I’m handing each patrol a three-by-five card with compass coordinates. You’ll have to use your compasses to find your campsite. Once you’ve set up camp, you can send somebody up to the food distribution center to pick up a chuck box and some food. The chuck box will have your stove and spices and things in it. You’ll be using it all week, so take good care of it.”

Brandon's mouth dropped open. "We have to cook our own breakfast?"

Jason laughed. "Yeah. And lunch. And dinner. We're pretty much on our own, guys. Each patrol has to fend for itself."

Tait pulled out his compass. "I'm a good cook, but I've never used my compass to find anything. How do we do that?"

"It's easy. Let's see the map coordinates they gave us." Jason studied the card for a moment and then shrugged. "Okay, first we have to go forty-five degrees for one-hundred-fifty paces. Look at your compass. See the little line-mark on the outside dial? You twist that around to the '45' and then turn your whole compass around until the floating needle lines up with this other mark in the middle. Then the arrow at the top of the compass points the way you should go."

Jason Francois outside his tent in the City Rats Patrol campsite

"Oh." Tait's stomach growled loudly. "Let's get started. I'm starving!"

Jason laughed. "Not so fast. First we have to pack

up our tents and stuff. You'd better tell your stomach it's going to be a while."

Once they were packed, Jason led the patrol off at a forty-five-degree angle, counting each step. The area was wild with thick trees and steep, rocky hillsides. They had to step over rocks and squeeze through bushes, but they finally made it to one-hundred-fifty paces. Next came three more directions. To their surprise, the last coordinate led them straight to a small clearing. It would be Patrol 8's campsite for the week.

"Home sweet home," Jason said, dropping his backpack. "This isn't bad at all. Let's get our camp set up so we can get some breakfast."

They pitched their tents and then hiked to the food distribution center to pick up their supplies. The assistant scoutmaster handed them a crate with eggs, pancake mix, syrup, and some powdered milk.

"Good luck," he said. "Try not to burn it. That's it until lunch."

Tait volunteered to cook, but the scoutmasters had assigned different cooks, clean-up people, and fire tenders for each day. Tait's turn to cook wouldn't come for a few days. That morning the pancakes tasted a little like smoke, and the eggs had a few black specks that were either ashes or gnats. But by then, they were all so hungry they didn't much care.

Devin shoved a forkful of pancake into his mouth. "So what's the deal with all these classes we have to go to today?" he asked. The syrup was dripping down his chin, but he snaked out his tongue to catch most of it.

"I heard we'll get to make water-balloon catapults later," BJ said.

Jason yawned. "I guess we'll just have to wait and see. We have a few minutes before the first class will start. Let's clean up and go look around."

They split up to explore the area. Jason picked a trail that led uphill, hoping to get a better view. Halfway up, he spotted some sun-bleached bones sticking out from under a bush. He used a stick to drag them out for a closer look. Enough were still sticking together to tell it had been a deer. He wondered what had attacked and eaten it. A bear? A wildcat? The teethmarks on the bones looked pretty big.

Returning to camp, he learned each patrol was supposed to pick a name and make a flag. It gave him an idea.

"I found some old deer bones up the trail," he said. "They're still kind of stuck together. If we hooked them onto a stick, they'd hang down like a flag. We could call ourselves the 'City Rats.' You know, like scavengers! It would be perfect."

John howled with laughter. "Let's do it!"

"Yeah!" Brandon chimed in. "All the other patrols are making these lame little flags with colored markers. Ours will be *bad!*"

They quickly tramped back up the trail and tied the bones to the end of a long, forked stick. When Jason lifted it in the air, the deer's ribcage and leg bones dangled down. They had their flag!

"Okay, City Rats!" he said with a grin. "Let's show the rest of these patrols how it's done!" Laughing, they marched down to their first leadership class, proudly holding their flag in front of them. The other scouts stared as they caught sight of the gruesome "flag" with its leg bones dancing in the breeze. The City Rats Patrol was soon known throughout the entire scout camp.

Camping by Patrol

The first leadership class lasted until lunchtime. Brandon was named the first patrol leader for the City Rats, so for the rest of that day he was supposed to be in charge. Jason watched with amusement as the younger boy nervously led their patrol back to their campsite for lunch.

It was going to be interesting taking orders from a thirteen-year-old! But that was the whole point—good leaders knew how to follow orders as well as give them. Jason kept his mouth shut, even when Brandon made mistakes. Brandon would learn. And if he didn't, they could always tie him to a tree and threaten to leave him there. It had been done before. Jason grinned at the thought.

That evening, after a long day of classes, the City Rats wearily returned to their campsite. It was off by itself, about two-hundred yards from the next nearest patrol. Still acting as leader, Brandon sent Jason and John off to gather rocks for their fire ring. Before they could build an open campfire, they had to dig a fire pit and surround it with rocks. That kept the flames from spreading out to the grass or dry pine needles.

Later, after cooking dinner, Jason glanced around at the other boys in his patrol. Their faces looked young in the flickering red firelight.

"We probably should get to bed pretty soon," he suggested. "We have to get up at six o'clock."

Tait and Matt exchanged impish grins, obviously not planning on sleeping anytime soon. Jason shook his head, suddenly feeling old. It was pretty bad when you'd rather sleep than sit up telling ghost stories around a campfire. But he knew what it felt like to get up in the morning after just two or three hours' sleep. It was like being run over by a truck or maybe beaten with a baseball bat—not good, not good at all.

"You guys suit yourself," he said mildly. "I'm turning in. I'll see you in the morning."

He unzipped his tent and crawled inside, zipping it again behind him to keep bugs out. As he unlaced his shoes, he thought back over the day. The classes had been kind of dull, but that's the way it always was in training camps. Sighing, he flopped down on his sleeping bag and rolled over to grope in his backpack for his flashlight and Bible. For the last year, he had made it a habit to read his Bible every night before bed. Sometimes he only read a verse or two, but other times, if it got interesting, he read more.

The pages fell open to the Book of John. He squinted at the fine print in the glare of the flashlight. *"My command is this: Love each other as I have loved you. Greater love has no one than this, that he lay down his life for his friends...."* Jason yawned again. His flashlight beam slid off the pages and danced around the inside of the tent. He decided he was too tired tonight to read. It had been a long day. He shoved the Bible back into his pack and flicked off the flashlight. He was asleep in seconds.

Over the days that followed, the routine stayed about the same. Up at six, salute the flag, cook and eat breakfast, go to classes, cook lunch, go to more classes. Even though the classes stayed boring, the boys got to joke around a lot in between. By the third or fourth night, the City Rats had made friends with the camp staff and many of the other patrols.

The staff was almost as bad as the scouts about playing pranks. One night, right after Jason turned off his flashlight, he heard heavy breathing outside his tent. Twigs snapped. Suddenly a loud, deep *rra-aa-ar!* exploded outside, followed by laughter. It was the staff, stalking around making bear noises. It scared several of the younger boys, but Jason knew who it was. He buried his head in his sleeping bag and ignored them.

On the fifth day, the City Rats were given projects to do. Each patrol had to build a gate, a wash rack, and a trash can using nothing but what they could find in the woods and in their camping gear. Almost everything ended up being made of sticks and rope. The City Rats' gate was funny looking, and their wash rack was lopsided, but their trash can was a work of art.

They had scrounged around until they found a bunch of straight sticks. Then, using their trusty scout knives, they had cut them all to the same length and tied them together into a trash can shape. They even made a lid. It didn't exactly fit, but it looked good. They were the only patrol with a trash can lid.

Jason was drifting off to sleep that night when he heard twigs snapping outside his tent again. His first thought was that the staff was up to their tricks again. This time though, the noise was different—quieter and more stealthy. There was no growling, no laughter. More twigs snapped. Something was walking past his tent, and it sounded big.

Jason lay still, trying not to get excited. Probably a dumb old bear, he thought. In the years since his first campout, he had been around other bears. Most of the time they stayed out of sight, just snooping around camp late at night.

Then he heard an odd snuffling sound just a few feet away. The bear was sniffing along the back edge of his tent! He held his breath, telling himself he was silly to be worried. If you didn't bother bears, they didn't bother you. They were usually scared of people.

Sure enough, the snuffling stopped. Slowly, the snapping sounds faded back into the dark woods. Smiling at himself, Jason rolled over and was soon snoring.

Catapults and Water Balloons

The next day more fun activities were planned. The big assignment for the day was to plan and make a water-balloon catapult. The following day, there would be a huge water-balloon war between the patrols. The City Rats planned to win.

"Here are the plans they gave us," said Jason, gathering the Rats in a tight circle. They stared down at the paper. It showed something that looked like a little seesaw with a cup on one end and a rope on the other. "We need to build our catapult and then test it using pine cones. That way we'll know how far it can shoot and how to aim it."

Tait nodded. "How does it work?"

"We build an A-frame stand and balance a flat stick or board across the top of it. We attach a cup to one end of the board to hold the water balloon and tie a rope to the other end. When we pull the rope, it launches the water balloon."

They got busy. When the catapult was finished, Tait gathered an armful of pine cones. BJ dropped a pine cone into the cup to try it out.

"Stand back!" he commanded. "We're gonna aim for that tree over there." He pointed to a tree about fifteen feet away. When he jerked the rope, however, the pine cone only flew about two feet before thudding to the ground. BJ laughed along with the others. Their catapult needed some work!

The next few tries didn't go much better. Once the pine cone flew straight up and came down on Matt's head; another time it flew backward and almost nailed Jason in the face. After a lot of experimenting, they were able to aim and shoot with at least some accuracy. They were ready for war! That afternoon, the scoutmaster announced that it was time to pack up for an overnight hike into the mountains. They would sleep under the stars, not in tents. Hopefully, it wouldn't rain.

Jason went back to his tent to roll his sleeping bag and clean up. He kept his tent a lot neater than he did his room at home. As he stuffed a clean change of clothes into his backpack, he thought briefly about the bear that had walked through camp the night before. If the bear came back tonight, he'd find an empty tent!

Jason just hoped the animal wouldn't be roaming around up on the dark mountainside where they would be camping. It wouldn't be much fun to wake up face-to-face with a bear if you were outside trapped in a sleeping bag!

The City Rats stayed together on the long hike that afternoon, laughing and talking. They were excited about the water-balloon war the next day. They would also play games, put on skits, and do other fun stuff to celebrate their last day in camp. After a whole week of classes, they deserved time off!

After dinner that night, each of the patrols elected a permanent patrol leader. They were supposed to pick their leader based on the job he had done all week. The City Rats unanimously chose Jason.

Friday morning came. Jason woke up early, excited at the thought of the day ahead. After breakfast the whole group hiked back down to camp. It was time to get ready for war!

Each patrol had to fill up their own water balloons. The trick was to make sure they were filled just right. If they were too full, they would break in midair; if they were too empty, they would bounce without breaking. It took skill and a lot of arguing to get them just right.

The scoutmasters made the patrols line up facing each other, like the battle lines in old Civil War movies. The City Rats confidently got in line with their catapult and a milk crate full of wobbly water balloons. With all their pine cone practice, how could they miss?

At the scoutmaster's signal, the City Rats jumped into action. With Jason in command, they quickly loaded a balloon onto their catapult and aimed at the line of boys across from them.

"Fire!" Jason yelled.

Tait jerked the rope. A bright blue water balloon shot straight up, paused, and then started back down at them. They scattered, trying not to get hit with their own balloon. It hit the ground and exploded, splashing all over them. Meanwhile, two other balloons whizzed past their heads.

"Hand me another balloon," Jason said. "The pine cones we practiced with must have been a lot lighter. We've got to figure out how to do it with balloons!"

The air was soon filled with water balloons and laughter. Two of the City Rats' balloons burst in their hands as they tried to load them. It wasn't long before all the boys were soaked. It was hard to tell which patrol was winning and which was losing. After the last water balloon exploded, each patrol claimed to have won. By then, it didn't much matter.

The rest of the day passed quickly. As the sun sank and the air grew cool again, the damp and weary City Rats returned to their camp to build one last campfire. It was hard to believe their week together was almost over.

Down for the Last Night

Sitting by the fire, Jason looked at his fellow patrol members with satisfaction. A week before they had all been strangers; now they were a team. That was the best part of Boy Scout camping trips. You always made new friends.

The two youngest boys, Tait and Brandon, had gained a lot of confidence. Brandon had turned into a pretty good cook, and Tait now used his compass like a pro. He's a nice kid, Jason thought. They all were.

By the time the fire burned low, they were getting sleepy. Jason finally stood up and stretched. "Well, I guess it's time to put out the fire, guys. We need to pack most of our stuff and start tearing down camp. We're leaving early in the morning."

They poured water on the fire and filled the fire pit with sand. Then they tore apart the fire ring and scattered all the rocks. The rule was to always leave a campsite looking like you'd never been there.

It was around nine-thirty when the last of the City Rats wandered off to bed. Tait and Brandon decided to sleep outside again, under the stars. They picked a spot out in the open, about twenty feet from Jason's and BJ's tents. Matt also decided to sleep outside, but he picked a spot away from the others. The rest of them zipped themselves snugly into their tents.

Jason, though tired, decided to sit up for a few minutes and read his Bible. He'd skipped the night before, while they were camping on the mountain. Aiming his flashlight at the pages, he started reading the Book of Job.

It told the depressing story about a good man who had terrible things happen to him. Job, a rich man with ten children, lost everything he had in a single day. His children were all killed. His property was destroyed or stolen. He got big, nasty sores all over his body. Then, right when he thought it couldn't possibly get worse, his best friends all turned their backs on him. Instead of helping him, they accused him of doing something bad to deserve it all!

Jason shook his head. Poor Job. It reminded him of the old saying, "With friends like that, who needs enemies?" Real friends were always there when you needed them. You could count on them no matter what.

The camp had grown quiet. But as he continued to read, he heard muffled voices and a low laugh outside. He grinned. The staff must be up to their tricks again. Any minute now, there would be another "bear" outside.

"Grr-rrr!" The low growl came from somewhere off to his left. They were probably outside BJ's tent.

"Hey, knock it off!" BJ said sleepily. "You guys woke me up!" Twigs snapped as the group moved off, probably to scare Jeremy or Devin. Distant screams and shrieks marked their progress through the different campsites. They were shaking some of the tents and grabbing some of the boys sleeping outside.

The camp grew quiet again. For some reason, Jason wasn't sleepy. He was still reading when he heard another noise outside. It sounded like his *real* bear visitor from the other night. He waited, marking its movements by the snapping of twigs. Like before, it snuffled at his tent and then kept going. Soon the camp was silent once again.

Five minutes later, Jason was about to click off his flashlight when he heard a high-pitched scream outside. It sounded like Tait or Brandon.

At first he thought the staff had sneaked back to

scare them. Sleeping outside like that, they were easy targets. But this time, the shrieks didn't end in giggles.

"Help me! Please help me!" someone cried again.

Still half-convinced it was a joke, Jason jumped up and slipped into his shoes. He kept his flashlight in his hand.

"*Jason!* Help me!" It was Tait.

Attacked!

At Tait's terrified scream, Jason knew for sure something was wrong. He burst out of his tent, his heart pounding. He swung his flashlight around, looking for Tait. What he saw froze him in place.

A four-hundred-pound black bear faced him across the small clearing, with Tait between them. Standing on all fours, it towered over Tait, who was sitting up in his sleeping bag. The boy's head was bleeding, and he was sobbing and screaming. As Jason watched in horror the bear pounced, sinking its teeth into the back of Tait's neck.

At that same moment, a shout came from a tent nearby. "Jason! Brandon's in here with me. He's hurt!" It was BJ.

"Give him first aid, and both of you stay in the tent!" Jason hadn't even noticed Brandon's empty sleeping bag. He must have gotten away when the bear first attacked.

But if Tait was to survive, Jason knew he would have to act fast. He ran a few steps closer to the bear, shining his flashlight into its face. It stared back at him, its dark eyes glinting like marbles. It still had Tait, kicking and screaming, clamped in its powerful jaws.

"Tait! Play dead! Do you hear me? Stop screaming and play dead!"

Instantly, Tait went limp. As he dangled from the bear's jaws, blood poured down his face and neck and dripped onto the ground. For a heart-stopping moment, Jason was afraid he wasn't acting. Then he saw the boy's frightened eyes turn to him.

"Don't worry, I'm not going to leave you," Jason said quietly. "I'll be right here. You're doing great."

Jason looked around quickly for a weapon. Seeing several big sticks on the ground, he scooped them up. When he held one up, the bear growled and pricked its ears sharply forward. Its fangs were now clamped halfway around Tait's head.

Jason took careful aim and then threw the stick as hard as he could. "Get out of here!" he yelled as it hit the animal in the side. "Go away! Get out!"

Startled, the bear dropped Tait and ran, muscles rippling under its thick black fur. But after just a few feet, it stopped and turned around. Before Jason could move, it lunged back to grab Tait again by the neck. This time it started dragging him off.

"Play dead, Tait!" Jason reminded him as the boy once again screamed. "I'm still here!"

As the bear dragged Tait across the clearing, Jason chased them. He threw another stick, but this time it hit Tait instead of the bear. The bear kept going, heading for the woods at the edge of camp.

Jason only had one more stick. Holding his breath, he aimed and threw it. This time it hit. The bear dropped Tait and moved away, looking confused.

"Go away!" Jason shouted, waving his arms. "Get out of here!"

In the moonlight, it looked like Tait's whole body was dark with blood. If he didn't get first aid soon, he could bleed to death. Jason started toward Tait, keeping a wary eye on the bear.

But the bear wasn't finished yet. It wheeled to rush at Tait again, this time clamping its teeth on his hand. Once again, it started dragging him toward the dark woods.

Empty-handed, Jason looked around frantically for something else to throw. Then he spotted one of the big rocks they'd scattered from the fire ring. He picked it up and threw it at the bear, not even taking time to aim. The bear had Tait almost to the edge of the trees.

The rock thudded hard against the bear's side. Grunting, it dropped Tait and plunged away into the woods, crashing its way through the thick underbrush. Jason ran over to help Tait, but the younger boy was already up and running. Jason ran just behind him, listening all the time for any sound that the bear might be returning.

But after only a few steps, Tait collapsed. Jason bent down to help him up when John and several of the other boys appeared beside them.

"I'll take him on my back," John offered. "Let's get him over to the next campsite. Brandon's hurt too, but it's mostly a scratch. BJ already bandaged it."

Devin, Matt, and the rest of the City Rats put Tait in the middle of their group and marched down the trail to the Patrol 5 campsite. It was in the opposite direction from where the bear had gone.

The members of Patrol 5 gasped when they saw Tait's injuries. The back of his head and neck were completely shredded, and his arm and hand were deeply bitten. Jason lifted him onto a picnic table and stretched him out.

"Somebody go tell the staff what's happened and call for an ambulance," he snapped. "And the rest of you, find me some sleeping bags to put over Tait. He's starting to shiver. I think he's going into shock."

The boys scrambled to do what they were told. A moment later they returned with a whole pile of sleeping bags. Jason covered Tait and then leaned down to talk to him.

"Hey, Tait, how ya doing?" he said. "You okay?"

Tait's face was pale, almost white. He had lost a lot of blood. "I guess," he said faintly. He mumbled something else and then closed his eyes. Jason glanced over at John; Tait was starting to lose it.

Keeping Tait Awake

"Tait? You've gotta stay with us. Don't go falling asleep right now. Talk to me, okay?"

Tait's eyes fluttered back open with an effort. "What?"

"I said talk to me. Do you remember my name?"

Tait almost smiled. "Jason," he said. "I forget your last name."

"That's okay. I forget your last name too."

When Tait tried to turn his head, Jason motioned for BJ to hold him still. If Tait's neck was broken or anything, moving it wrong could leave him paralyzed. Jason knew it was always best to keep injured necks straight.

Soon the whole camp staff came running down to the campsite. The scoutmaster said they'd called the ambulance and an AirVac unit. The camp had a helicopter pad nearby; Tait would get to the hospital quicker by air.

Jason and the others kept Tait talking. "I woke up when Brandon yelled," Tait recalled when they asked him about what happened. "I looked up, and there was this giant bear standing over me. I remembered you were supposed to act like a rock, so I just laid there, pretending not to see it. But it grabbed my sleeping bag and started pulling me along the ground." He paused and fell silent.

"Tait!" Jason said sharply. "Stay with us. What happened next?"

"Well, it just kept pulling me toward the woods. I finally grabbed a tree and held on, but it kept going until it pulled my sleeping bag halfway off. It wasn't going to stop. I was afraid it was going to drag me into the trees, and nobody would know. That's when I decided I'd better start yelling. The minute I yelled, it started biting and clawing me."

"You probably did the right thing. We'd never have been able to find you in the woods." Jason patted Tait's arm gently. "I'm just impressed that you could play dead like that while it was chewing on you. That's what really saved your life, you know. If you'd gotten hysterical and kept fighting, I think it would've killed you right there. That took a lot of guts."

Fifteen minutes later the ambulance arrived. The EMTs took care of Tait and checked out Brandon. Finally, they turned to Jason.

"Are you okay?" one of them asked. "You look kind of pale. You'd better let me take your pulse."

Jason held out his wrist. Even now, when it was all over, his heart was still pounding like crazy. He hadn't realized until that very moment how scared he had been.

The helicopter came and took Tait to the hospital. After he left, the staff decided all the patrols should sleep in the Patrol 5 campsite the rest of the night for safety. Nobody wanted to take a chance on running into a hungry, bloodthirsty bear in the dark.

Most of the boys eventually fell asleep, but Jason

didn't. Lying there in the dark, he remembered the look in the bear's eyes, and in Tait's. Looking back, it was probably stupid of him to have chased the bear like that. But he hadn't known what else to do. He couldn't just stand there and let it chew Tait's head off right in front of him. Tait had been counting on him.

That's what friends were for.

Remembering the Rescue

The next morning, the local sheriff came by to fill out a report about what had happened. Jason and Brandon walked him back over to the City Rats' campsite to show him how it had started.

"Tait and I were sleeping outside, right here," Brandon explained, pointing to the spot. "Then something stepped on me and woke me up. I looked up and saw something big kind of walking over me. It scratched my side. I jumped up and ran to BJ's tent."

The sheriff nodded. "We're going to have to hunt the bear down now and kill it. Once they cross the line and attack a human like that, they're dangerous. They start looking at people as food."

From that point, Jason picked up the story. He told how he heard Tait screaming and ran out to see the bear chewing on his neck. He walked the sheriff through the whole thing, right up to where the bear had dragged Tait to the edge of the bushes.

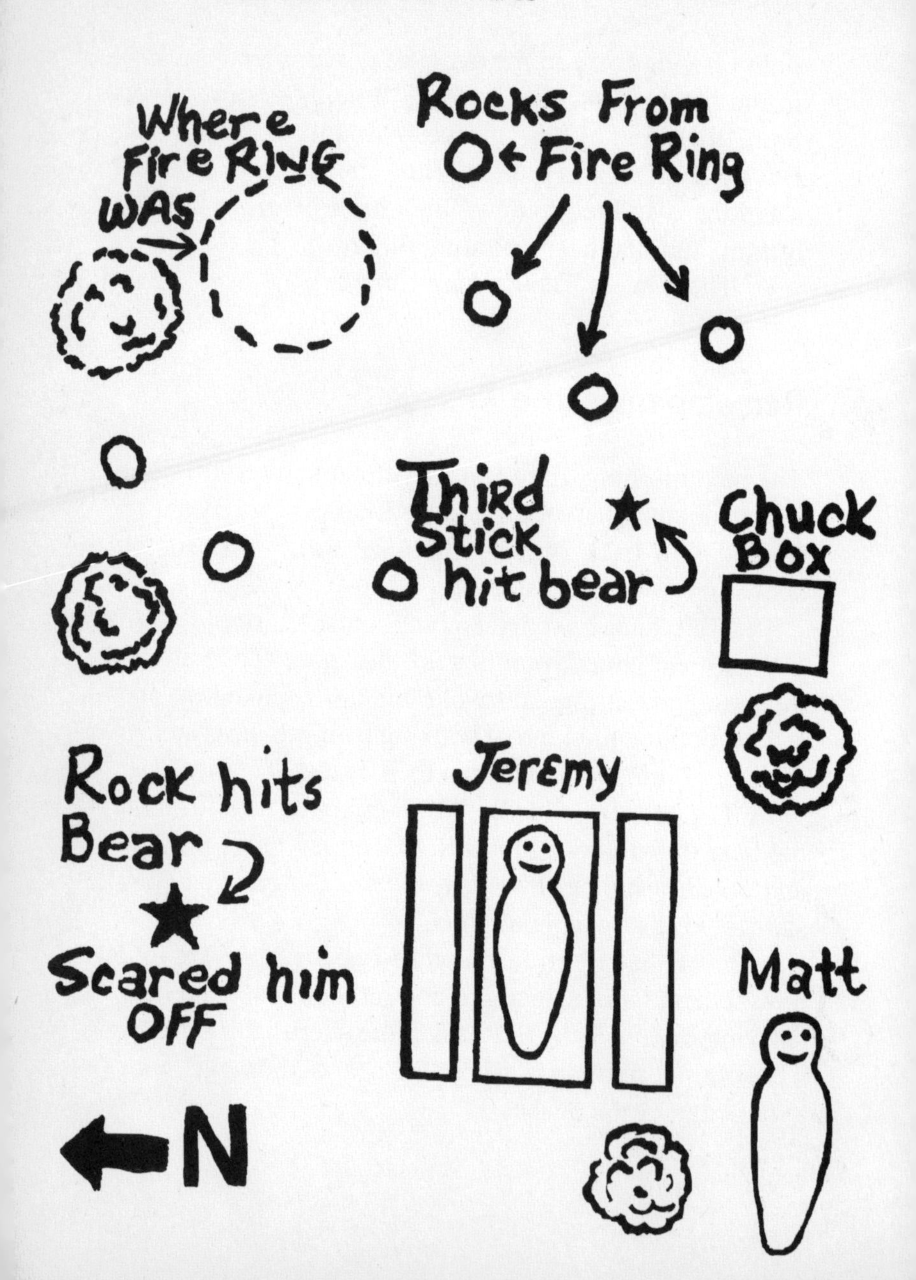
Where Fire Ring WAS
Rocks From Fire Ring
Third Stick hit bear
Chuck Box
Jeremy
Rock hits Bear
Scared him OFF
Matt
N

Devin's Tent
Second stick hits bear
First stick hits bear
Patrol Flag
Tait
BJ's Tent
Brandon
Three Sticks
The BIG Bear
My Tent

"I was afraid once it got Tait in the woods I'd never be able to follow them. I grabbed a big rock and threw it." He smiled; the rock he had thrown was still lying there. He bent down to pick it up.

"*This* rock," he said. "It's what finally scared the bear off."

The sheriff smiled. "You did a good job. Not that it was smart, mind you. That bear might've just dropped the boy and attacked you. You wouldn't have had much chance against 400 pounds of muscles, claws, and fangs."

Jason shrugged. "I didn't really think about it much at the time. I just knew I couldn't leave Tait. He's my friend."

The sheriff patted his shoulder. "Well, I think he's a lucky boy to have a friend like you."

After the sheriff left, Jason packed up his gear and loaded it back into his car. Then he went back to the City Rats' campsite for one last look around.

Now it was just a small, empty clearing in the woods. The only trace left of the City Rats was their patrol flag, posted at the edge of camp. Jason walked over and pulled the flagpole out of the ground, making the deer bones clatter. He smiled. It was definitely the best flag in camp!

He held it for a moment, thinking back over the last week. This was always the hard part, realizing it was all over. A few of the City Rats might keep in touch, but they would never be a patrol together again.

He looked up at the dangling bones one more time

and then deliberately smashed them against a tree. They fell to the ground in a broken heap. With a sigh, he started the hike back to his car.

Back Home Again

"So how was camp? Did you have fun?" Mrs. Francois followed Jason back and forth as he lugged in his camping gear. "Did anything exciting happen?"

"I don't want to talk about it, Mom." Jason dropped his backpack on the floor. "Maybe later."

Mrs. Francois's eyebrows went up. "Why? Did something bad happen?"

"I don't want to talk about it."

His mother crossed her arms. "Jason Francois, you tell me what's going on right now. Did you get in a wreck or something? I was worried about you driving that whole way by yourself."

"I didn't get in a wreck."

Sighing, Jason went to the kitchen to get a drink. Mrs. Francois followed. Jason finally gave up and sat down across the table from her.

"First you have to promise not to get upset," he started. That was the wrong thing to say. His mother's eyes got wide and she started breathing hard. Jason decided it would be better just to blurt it out. "Okay, Mom, the thing is, a bear attacked one of the kids in my patrol, and I had to scare it off."

"A *bear?* A real bear?"

"Yes. It looked like a black bear. It wandered into our camp while everybody except me was sleeping and attacked a kid named Tait. He was sleeping outside."

"Was he hurt?"

"Yeah, pretty bad. A helicopter took him to the hospital last night. The bear kind of grabbed him by the head and was chewing on him. It kept trying to drag him off into the woods."

He started to add an interesting bear fact—that bears don't like to eat fresh meat. They usually kill stuff and hide it so it'll rot a little before they eat it. But Jason decided this wasn't the time to tell his mom about bears' eating habits.

"And you—What did you do?"

"Tait was screaming for me to help him. I ran out and started throwing things at the bear and yelling at it. It ran off a couple of times, but it kept coming back and grabbing Tait again. I think it already had the taste of his blood."

Oops! Jason realized instantly he'd said something else wrong. His mother looked sick.

"You mean to tell me," she said faintly, "that you were *yelling* at a bear and throwing things at it?"

"Yeah, pretty much. It kept dragging Tait away, so I had to keep chasing it. I didn't want it to get him into the woods."

"Chasing it. You were *chasing* it? How big was it?"

"Pretty big. But Mom—"

"Are you *crazy?* You don't go around chasing bears! You run the other direction! What if it had turned on you? You could have been killed!"

Jason let her go on for a few minutes until she got it all out of her system. Then he said quietly, "Mom, that bear would've killed Tait if I hadn't done something. Tait's just a kid; he's only twelve. I couldn't run the other way and leave him like that. It wouldn't have been right."

Mrs. Francois said weakly, "Couldn't you have let somebody else do it? One of the scoutmasters or something?"

"None of them were around right then." Jason gave her a reassuring smile. "Besides, I had just been reading about how Job's friends deserted him just when he needed them most. I wasn't going to do that, Mom. I'd lay down my life for a friend if I had to. I was ready."

Mrs. Francois leaned over to hug him. "Well, *I'm* not ready to give you up yet. Don't you ever do that again, you hear me?"

Jason grinned. "Okay, Mom. The very next time I see a wild bear attacking somebody, I'll make sure to stay out of it. Scout's honor."

The Rest of the Story

Tait had to have his head, neck, and arms stitched up. He ended up with about eighteen staples as well as dozens of stitches.

After Tait got out of the hospital, Jason went to visit him. He took Tait an interesting souvenir: the rock that had finally scared off the bear. Jason had kept it after showing it to the sheriff.

"Thanks," Tait said, turning the rock over in his hands. "Thanks for everything, Jason."

"Don't worry about it. You would've done the same for me."

A few months later the Boy Scouts of America awarded Jason Francois the Honor Medal for Bravery—the highest award in the Boy Scouts.

One year after the attack, Jason earned the rank of Eagle Scout. New Eagle Scouts are recognized at a special ceremony called a Court of Honor, and the scout's friends and family are invited to attend. Tait and his family drove down from Tucson to attend Jason's ceremony.

At the end of the ceremony, Tait stepped forward to give Jason a special award: a glass trophy case containing a small photo of Tait and the rock Jason had used to save his life.

"I want you to have this back," Tait told him. "This rock is more your souvenir than mine. I don't need it to remember what you did. You're a real friend."

Tait Holbrook presents Jason Francois
with a memento of their unforgettable
"bear" adventure.

Tornado

The Adam DeSutter and Tim Boe Story

Above: Tim Boe (left) and Adam DeSutter at age 11, watching Plainfield High School football practice

"Hit him, Chris!"

"Come on, Fred! You can take him!"

Cheered on by a noisy crowd of ten- and eleven-year-olds, two angry, red-faced boys swung at each other. Adam DeSutter and Tim Boe stood at the back of the crowd, cheering for their friend Chris. Suddenly, they were interrupted by an angry shout. "Hey, you boys break it up!"

The old guy who lived in the house behind them had stepped outside to yell at them. He didn't look happy. "Go on!" he shouted, shaking his fist. "Get away from my yard!"

Tim jabbed Adam with his elbow. "Let's go."

The two boys had been best friends since they were six years old. They were a lot alike: both skinny with long legs, big ears, and short haircuts. Their dads were both football coaches at Plainfield High School, and they each had a big brother on the Plainfield Wildcats team. They had practically grown up together on the football field. They might have looked like brothers except that Tim was blond and Adam had dark hair.

Now, in the middle of August, it was almost time for school to start again in Illinois. Adam and Tim would be starting their first year of junior high.

Adam was just climbing on his bike when Joey, a short boy with dark hair, sauntered up and shoved him.

"I see your friend Chris quit," he sneered. "*You* wanna fight?"

Adam didn't really want to, but he couldn't back off from a big mouth like Joey. "I guess," he said.

Tim stepped up beside him. "You fight Adam, you'll have to fight me too," he said. He and Adam always stuck together. Besides, the other boy was two years older than both of them.

Joey sneered harder. "Fine. I can take on both of you at once!"

Hearing there might be another fight, some of the boys who had begun to leave started drifting back. "Let's go over behind the church," Mike suggested. "We can use our bikes to make a boxing ring for you guys."

Adam and Tim looked at each other. They knew if their moms caught them fighting in the churchyard, they were going to get killed. But what choice did they have?

"Fine," Tim said, answering for both of them. "Let's go."

There was an empty field next to the Bible Baptist Church down the street. The boys pedaled and bumped their way over the grass beside the church and then parked their bikes in a big circle. Adam, Tim, and Joey climbed into the middle of the ring.

Matt spat on the ground. "Ready?" he asked. "Okay, get 'em, Joey!"

Joey lunged forward, his fingers curled to claw Tim's face. Adam stepped in to sink his fist into Joey's stomach. Howling with pain, Joey kicked Adam's feet out from under him. As Adam fell, Tim knocked Joey down right beside him. Soon all three boys were thrashing around in the grass making grunting sounds.

But Joey didn't have a chance against Adam and Tim together. They were scrawny but tough. It wasn't long before they had Joey pinned down, half-sitting on him. They avoided his feet as he kicked and sputtered.

"You had enough?" Tim asked, panting.

"No!" Joey said defiantly. "I'm gonna kick both of you!"

Seeing that his hero was beaten, Matt stepped into the ring. "Hey, come on, Joey," he said. "Let these two babies go. You got somebody else to fight, remember?"

"Oh, yeah," Joey said. He looked relieved. "I almost forgot. Let me up, you guys."

Adam and Tim rolled their eyes. Matt was just trying to give his friend an easy way out. "I don't think so," Tim said. "Not until you say you give up."

Matt hissed something under his breath and then grabbed Tim's shoulder. "Let him go. I've got on baseball spikes. I might just have to kick you with them."

Tim looked up at Matt. He was big, *really* big, and his baseball spikes looked pretty sharp. It might be a good time to cooperate after all. Tim slowly stood up and brushed the grass off his pants.

"Okay, but don't try pushing us around again, or next time we'll have to teach you a lesson."

"Yeah, right," Joey said nastily. "I'm really scared."

Standing shoulder to shoulder, Tim and Adam glared as Joey rode off with his small group of friends. As soon as the other boys were out of sight, Tim and Adam broke into grins and high-fived each other.

"All right!" Adam said. "I guess we showed them, huh?"

"Yeah, but we'd better get out of here before the pastor or somebody catches us. I don't want to get into trouble. Want to go back to my house for some lunch?"

Summertime Game Plan

The Boes lived in Joliet, a ten-minute drive from the DeSutters' house in Plainfield. That morning Coach DeSutter had dropped Adam off at Tim's house before he went to football practice. Often, the two boys went along to watch, but this time they weren't in the mood. Since Adam lived just down the street from Plainfield High School, he could go there whenever he wanted.

They ate lunch and then wandered into the living room. Tim flopped down in his dad's recliner. Adam sprawled on the couch, letting his legs dangle sideways off the edge. They were both dirty and grass-stained from rolling around with Joey. Luckily, Mrs. Boe hadn't asked any questions,

Tim picked up the TV remote and quickly flipped through the channels. A soap opera…a talk show…a game show…a talk show…*another* talk show. Disgusted, he clicked off the TV. There was never anything good on TV during the day!

In the sudden silence, Adam sighed. "I can't believe it's only another week until school starts. Are you nervous about starting junior high?"

"Sort of," Tim replied. "How about you?"

"Sort of. I'm not looking forward to getting picked on all the time again. It was fun this last year to be in the highest grade."

"Yeah. Well, maybe it won't be so bad."

School—except for P.E.—had never been at the top of their lists of "Fun Things to Do." They would rather spend every day out on the basketball court or football field. They both planned to be professional football players when they grew up.

Adam suddenly laughed. "Wouldn't it be nice if somebody would open a Football School? My mom says I learned to count at football games by counting points. You could have Football Math, Football English, Football Science. It'd be a lot more fun than sitting in classrooms."

Tim grinned. "Then at P.E., I guess you'd go out and play football, huh?"

"Sure!" Adam said. "What else?"

"Sounds good to me. Maybe we could talk our dads into starting a school like that someday."

Adam shook his head. "I don't think it'll ever happen. It would be too much fun. Teachers like to torture kids."

It was almost three o'clock before Coach DeSutter and Coach Boe showed up. They both looked hot and tired.

Coach DeSutter was a big, tall man with graying hair and glasses. "Come on, Adam!" he called, sticking his head in the front door.

On the way out, Adam asked Tim, "You gonna come to practice in the morning with your dad?"

"Yeah, I guess. There's nothing to do around here."

"I'll meet you then. Maybe we can play in the gym."

"Okay. See ya!"

Adam followed his dad out to their car, the hot summer sun beating down on his back. His father's shirt was soaked with sweat. Practice must have been murder in that heat!

"What did you and Tim do today?" Coach DeSutter asked after they got in the car.

"Just rode bikes and stuff." Adam kind of skipped over the fight in the churchyard. What his father didn't know couldn't get him in trouble. "How did practice go?"

Coach DeSutter lifted his baseball cap, smoothed his hair back, and then yanked the cap back down. "It went okay. Kevin did a good job." Kevin was Adam's big brother. He played quarterback. "I just wish it wasn't so hot."

"How'd Eric play?" Eric was Tim's big brother. This was his first season on the team.

"Great," Coach DeSutter said. "I think he's going to be a good player."

The DeSutters lived in a red and white two-story house. The neighborhood kids called it the "pillar house" because it had four tall, white pillars across the front.

Coach DeSutter pulled into the driveway and then inched the car into the garage, trying hard not to run over any of the stuff jammed in there. The garage was full of interesting things: an old wooden dresser, a refrigerator, a portable basketball goal, and a half-dead plant, not to mention bicycles, golf clubs, and lawn tools. It was always hard to find room for their cars.

In the summer heat, the garage felt like an oven. Adam got out and hurried into the house. "Mom, we're home!" he called, letting the icy air conditioning curl around him like a cool sheet.

His mother's voice drifted back to him from the living room. "I'm in here!" she called. She smiled when Adam walked in. "How was it at Tim's house today?"

"Fine. What's for dinner?"

"Hamburgers. But you'd better go take a shower first. You stink. Don't sit down on anything."

Adam sniffed his underarm. "I don't smell *that* bad, do I?"

Mrs. DeSutter's eyes twinkled behind her glasses. "Yes," she said firmly. "Go get cleaned up!"

Life at their house was usually pretty relaxed. Kevin's friends on the football team were always tramping in and out, joking with Coach DeSutter and eating everything in the refrigerator. Sometimes Adam got to play basketball with them out in the driveway. It made him feel big to play with all the high school guys.

He got up the next morning in time to go with his father to football practice. The school was only three blocks away, but he didn't feel like walking. He hoped Tim would remember to show up.

Practice at Plainfield

Plainfield High School was a big, sprawling building made of red bricks. It had some one-story parts and some two-story parts, all with flat roofs. The football field and bleachers were off to one side right across from the main gym.

Coach DeSutter parked beside the gym. Billy, a quarterback, was waiting with some other players. Adam spotted Billy's brand-new Geo Storm parked off to one side all by itself. It was a shiny teal green. Adam smiled. "Billy really loves his new Storm, doesn't he?" he mused aloud. "I wonder what he'd do if the football hit it and dented it. He'd probably cry or something."

Coach DeSutter smiled. "I doubt *that,* but he might take whoever dented it and throw them clear across the field!"

Coach Boe pulled up in his truck a few minutes later. Tim was with him. Adam ran over. "Hi. I was hoping you were still gonna come."

"Uh-huh." Tim yawned. "I'm not very awake, but I'm here. So what do you want to do?"

"I don't know. What do you want to do?"

Matt, a lineman on the team, walked past just then and whacked Adam on the side of the head. "Hi, rat," he greeted him cheerfully. "Hi, little Boe. What're you guys up to?"

Adam rubbed his head. "Nothing much. How about you?"

"Not much. See you guys later!"

The boys watched Matt join the other players walking out to the field. "That hurt," Adam complained, still rubbing his head.

Tim shrugged. "At least he didn't make us carry

his pads or send us off on some stupid errand." The players were nice to them most of the time, but sometimes they treated them like personal slaves. They sent them to get drinks or made them lug around equipment. But Adam and Tim usually didn't mind. They liked feeling like they were part of the team.

Once the players headed out to the field, the two younger boys slipped into the school's side door. They weren't really supposed to mess around in the gym during football practice, but what would somebody do if they caught them, send them to School Jail?

"You want to go to the big gym or the small gym?" Adam asked. The main gym was down the hall to their left; the small gym was down some steps to their right.

"Let's go to the small gym first. We can play on the ropes."

The long, knotted ropes dangling down in the small gym were good for swinging or climbing. Adam ran inside and grabbed one. With a wild yell, he ran as fast as he could and then jumped. He went skimming across the gym like Tarzan.

"C'mon, Tim!" he called as he whizzed past his friend. "This is fun!"

Tim grabbed one of the other ropes and started climbing like a monkey. Soon he was up near the ceiling. "Adam!" he yelled, touching the steel bar at the top. "Look at this!"

"Uh-huh." Adam was still swinging back and forth. "Hey, I have an idea. Let's stack up all the exercise mats and jump on them!"

"Okay." Tim quickly slid back down. He and Adam soon made a kind of mat mountain. "Now watch this!" Adam said. He backed up and then ran at the mats as fast as he could. He waited until the last minute to jump. Sailing through the air with his arms and legs sticking out in every direction, he looked like a flat, flying spider. He landed on his stomach and bounced a couple times.

Tim laughed. "My turn!" Instead of spider-jumping like Adam, he made bicycling motions in the air and landed sitting down.

They kept mat-diving until they got bored and then took turns burrowing down into the mats. One of them would wiggle in between the mats until he disappeared and then lay there while the other one jumped up and down on top of the stack. They wanted to see if it would break their legs or anything. It didn't.

When they got tired of that, they decided to play spies. They liked sneaking around the empty building, jumping out, and "shooting" each other. There were lots of places to hide, like the weight rooms and locker rooms.

Adam waited in the small gym, giving Tim time to run and hide. He counted to twenty and then edged out into the hallway. He pressed his back against the wall, trying not to make any noise. To win, he had to sneak up on Tim and then shoot him without warning.

The hallway was shaped like a big L. The main gym was straight ahead where the hallway made a sharp turn to the right. To reach that corner he would have to pass three "danger" areas on his left: the side door they had come in and the two weight room doorways. Tim could be hiding in any of them.

Adam slid along the wall, holding his "gun" up against his chest. He cocked an eye around the corner when he reached the side door. Tim wasn't there. He darted across the doorway and kept going.

It wasn't until he reached the second weight room doorway that a small figure suddenly leaped out at him from the shadows. He gasped, aiming his gun.

"Pow! *Pow-pow-pow!* Got you, Tim!"

"No, you didn't. I fired first. You're dead."

Adam shrugged. "Let's play again, only this time you count."

After three or four more spy games, they decided to walk back to Adam's house. They cut across the front of the school and started down the sidewalk, talking and laughing. They decided they would cool off for a while and then play a couple games of basketball.

Mrs. DeSutter was waiting when they walked in the front door. "Hi, Tim," she said in a friendly voice. In a less friendly voice, she asked Adam, "Didn't your father tell you yesterday to pick up the crab apples in the front yard? They make our yard look really bad!"

Adam gave Tim a look that said, "Mothers!" "Uh, I guess so, Mom. I just didn't have time."

"Well, you have the time now. Get busy and get them all out of the yard."

"I'll help," Tim offered. "Come on, Adam."

Once outside, Adam kicked a green crab apple across the yard. "I hate these things," he said. "I always get stuck picking them up."

"What are we supposed to do with them?"

"Throw them away. I'll get a bucket to put them in."

Adam went into the garage and snatched an old paint bucket off the shelves. Then he spotted his dad's golf clubs. It gave him an idea.

"Tim, c'mere!" he called. "Maybe we can make this a little more fun. Let's each take one of these golf clubs."

Tim grinned. "I don't think your mom's gonna like this, Adam."

"She just said to get them out of the yard. She didn't say *how* to get them out of the yard!"

Back outside, Adam carefully aimed his club at one of the hard, marshmallow-sized crab apples. "Fore!" he yelled, whacking it as hard as he could. It went sailing out into the street. It hit the pavement and bounced, only looking a little squished.

"Okay, you try it now. Let's take turns and see how far we can hit them."

Tim whacked his crab apple into the street about three houses away. Then it was Adam's turn again. He lined up on an apple, nailed it as hard as he could, and then flinched as it sailed straight across the street into their neighbor's yard.

"Oops," he said. He almost sounded scared.

"Oops?"

"That's Doc's house." Doc was a tall, white-haired man with thick glasses and lots of energy. His yard was always perfect, and he spent hours each day working to make sure it stayed that way. When neighborhood kids were foolish enough to step on his grass or pick his flowers, he would burst outside yelling. He didn't seem to like kids much. He had a nervous habit of jingling the change in his pockets when he talked. He made Tim nervous.

Luckily, Doc hadn't been looking out his window. Adam decided to stop playing crab apple golf and toss the rest of the fruit into the bucket.

"You know what really bugs me?" he griped as he scooped up a slightly rotten apple. "I can pick up every crab apple out here, but tomorrow they'll be all over the ground again." He pointed up into the branches of the crab apple tree. "See all those apples still hanging up there, just waiting to fall? I hate this tree."

"Maybe lightning will strike it," Tim suggested.

"Not with my luck. It'll probably keep growing and growing, making *thousands* of these stupid apples. And you watch, I'll have to pick up every single one. Just because I'm the youngest kid, I get stuck with all the chores."

"It's the same at my house. Eric's almost never home, so I have to take out the trash and help Dad clean the garage, stuff like that. I can't wait until I can drive. I'll stay gone all the time too."

Adam grinned. "I wonder what our moms will do when they don't have us at home to use as slaves?"

"Probably boss the dogs," Tim said. They both cracked up.

Last Days of Freedom

School was supposed to start the next Wednesday. That Tuesday, Adam woke up and stumbled downstairs to the kitchen. There was a note for him on the counter.

> *Adam—I have school today.* (Mrs. DeSutter taught second grade at Milne Grove Elementary School. Elementary school started one day earlier than junior high.) *Remember to empty the dishwasher. I'll be home around 3:30.*
>
> *Love, Mom*

Adam sighed. His last day of freedom, and as usual he was stuck with chores. He wadded up the note and threw it at the trash can. The dishwasher could wait until he was good and ready.

Coach DeSutter was at Plainfield High all day for teachers' meetings. Football practice wouldn't begin until three o'clock that afternoon. Tim was supposed to come to practice again.

The day dragged by for Adam. He watched TV and then went out to shoot some hoops. He thought a few times about emptying the dishwasher, but he wasn't *that* bored. Maybe if he waited long enough the Dish Fairy would surprise him and do it for him.

But by two-thirty he was too bored to stay home any longer. He headed for school, riding his scooter. He hadn't ridden it for a while. He liked the bump-bump-bump sound as he ran over the sidewalk cracks.

The sky was bright blue, the sun scorching down. It burned his scalp right through his short, stubbly hair. For once, he was glad not to be on the high school football team. They were going to die, practicing out in this heat!

He was still a long way off when he spotted Tim's flourescent green tank top. Tim was standing by the bleachers, talking to a couple of the football players. Seeing Adam, he looked up and waved.

Adam rode his scooter down the school's long driveway and stopped next to Tim. They found a little slice of shade outside the main gym and both sat down.

Adam wiped his sweaty forehead. "Can you believe how hot it is? I thought it was bad last week, but it must be a hundred degrees today."

"Somebody said it's ninety-seven," Tim said. "So what do you want to do?"

"I don't know. What do you want to do?" They both laughed. Neither of them liked making decisions.

"It's too hot to hang around here. Want to go back to my house? We can play basketball in the garage where it's shady. You can ride my scooter if you want. I'd rather walk."

"Okay, thanks!"

Walking and scootering together down the sidewalk, they talked about school. They couldn't believe it was going to start the very next day.

"Maybe there'll be another teachers' strike like last year," Tim said hopefully. "Remember? They shut down all the schools for a couple weeks."

Adam shook his head. "I don't think it's gonna happen this year. My dad hasn't said anything about a strike."

Tim squinted up into the sun. Sweat dotted his forehead. "Yeah. The junior high called my mom in today to substitute for a secretary. I guess school's gonna start on time."

They raided Adam's refrigerator and then went out to the garage. Adam opened the garage door but kept the small basketball hoop inside, out of the sun. He let Tim have the first shot. Before long they were yelling and zigzagging all around the garage in a game of one-on-one.

They had been playing for about thirty minutes when they heard a low rumbling noise. It sounded like thunder, but when they looked outside, the sky was still a clear, bright blue. A few minutes later they heard it again. This time the noise was louder.

Adam dribbled the ball out onto the driveway and squinted up at the sky. He didn't see anything, but he couldn't see much of the sky because of the trees and houses on both sides.

Tim walked out past him to the end of the driveway. “Hey, Adam, come look at this!” He pointed back over the top of Adam’s house.

Adam trotted out to join him. His eyes grew wide when he saw the thick black clouds rolling across the sky toward them, almost tumbling over each other. When thunder rumbled again, the sound seemed to go on forever.

“That looks weird,” he said. “I’ve never seen anything like that before.”

Tim was uneasy. “It looks like a bad storm’s coming. Want to go back up to the school?” Thunderstorms had always made him a little nervous. He would rather be at the school with his dad and Coach DeSutter than alone at Adam’s house.

Lightning streaked down, followed by a deafening *cr-ra-ack* of thunder. Adam jumped and then turned to toss the basketball back into the garage. “Let’s go!” he said. He wasn’t exactly crazy about storms either. He didn’t stop to close the garage door.

Chased by a Storm

They started down the sidewalk together at a fast trot. A cold gust of wind hit Adam’s neck. Surprised, he glanced back over his shoulder. The churning wall of black clouds behind them was huge and dark as night. The sky was also turning a funny greenish color.

"Come on!" Adam had never seen the sky look like that before. It kind of scared him.

They were about halfway to the school when it started hailing. Marble-sized chunks of ice fell and bounced on the sidewalk. Adam was amazed. "Look, it's raining ice!" he yelled.

Tim laughed. "It's *hail,* stupid! Haven't you ever seen hail before?"

"No!" Adam stopped and peered up at the sky. How could ice be falling from the sky in the middle of the summer? He yelped when an icy chunk nailed him in the eye.

But even hail couldn't distract them for long. The strange black clouds almost seemed to be following them. Every time they looked back, the clouds were bigger and closer. The thunder had become one long roar. Oddly enough, the sky in front of them was still bright blue and sunny.

The boys were both relieved when they got to Plainfield High. They cut across the parking lot and ducked between the school and the stadium by the main gym.

Coach DeSutter and Coach Boe were standing at the school's side door, waving all the players inside. Between the varsity and junior varsity teams, there were 107 players in all. They were still streaming in from the field, many of them laughing as hail bounced off their helmets.

"Hurry up!" Coach DeSutter shouted. "Take off your cleats before you go in. Don't mark up the gym floor!"

Adam edged his way along the outside wall of the main gym, laughing as hail bounced off Tim's head. Now that he was with his father, he felt much more confident. The gym wall blocked his view of the strange black clouds that had been following them.

"Hey, Dad!" he called. "I got hit in the eye by a piece of hail!"

"I guess you should be inside then," Coach DeSutter said sharply. He turned to yell at some players still clowning around out in the field. "Move it, you guys! We've got lightning! Get inside!"

Out of the corner of his eye, Adam saw Billy's Geo Storm parked over by Coach Boe's truck. Could hail dent cars? Tim had run over to his father, who was busy herding the rest of the team inside. A group of players was bunched up next to the building, ducking hail as they tried to pull off their cleats.

Adam dove through the doorway, trying not to get trampled by the older boys. Tim followed a moment later. They glanced around trying to decide what to do. The girls' volleyball team was in the main gym warming up for a game. Most of the football players were crowded around the door waiting to see if the storm would blow over. Adam spotted Kevin across the crowd and waved.

Once the last player was inside, Coach DeSutter closed the door. He peered out through the narrow glass pane. "Doesn't look too great," he said gloomily. "Did the weather report say anything about hail?"

"Nope," Coach Boe replied. "It said there might be a few thunderstorms this afternoon, but that was it."

The rain and hail pounded noisily on the roof, almost drowning out the thunder. Despite the swirling rain, the sky over the football field was still bright. There was no sign of the churning black clouds.

Adam didn't like standing around. He nudged Tim. "Want to go play in the gym until it clears up?"

Tim shrugged. They trotted down the steps together, glad to get out of the crowded hallway. Ed, Matt, Ben, and a few other players were in the small gym. They waved as the younger boys walked in and then went back to laughing and talking. Adam and Tim went over to play on the ropes, but Tim soon grew restless.

"I want to see what the storm's doing," he said. "I'm going back upstairs."

Disaster Approaches

Less than two miles away, a roaring nightmare of swirling black was nearing Plainfield. Huge trees were yanked from the ground like weeds and then sucked thousands of feet up into the air. Cars were picked up and crushed like toys. Houses blew apart. Roaring like a freight train, the dark mass exploded everything in its path.

It was a monster tornado, seven hundred feet wide with winds over two hundred fifty miles per hour. Now, traveling at more than one hundred miles per hour, it was sweeping straight toward Adam's neighborhood—and Plainfield High School.

"Dad? What's it doing out there?" Tim shoved his way over to his father's side. Most of the players had either wandered down the hall to the weight rooms or had gone to stand in the longer hallway outside the main gym. There was only a small crowd still gathered by the door.

"About the same," Coach Boe said. "I don't think it's going to let up. I just hope it's not like this tomorrow. The first day of school is hard enough without bad weather."

"Yeah," Tim said. He stepped closer to the door and stared out through the glass. The clouds still weren't very dark, but they had funny waves in them. He frowned. Had they looked like that before? As he watched, a heavy stadium chair blew off the press box above the bleachers and disappeared. Then a tall tree, whipped by the wind, suddenly bent sideways until it was almost touching the ground.

"Dad!" he said excitedly. "Did you see that?"

At that moment the lights went out.

The tornado was now half a mile from the high school. There was still no warning, no alarm. The killer winds had come out of nowhere to strike with deadly force.

This storm was truly a monster, bigger and more

powerful than a normal tornado. Instead of having one funnel, a whirlpool made of wind, it had five: four smaller funnel clouds revolving around one larger one—like the rotating blades of an electric shaver, all spinning side by side—five tornados in one.

Seconds later, the winds ripped into Adam's neighborhood. Roofs were ripped off and blew away. Windows exploded. Walls collapsed. Cars were picked up and thrown blocks away. Trees were flattened, broken off at the ground.

At Adam's house, three of the tall white pillars were yanked away by the wind. The tall crab apple tree bent and then broke. Splintered branches flew like deadly spears into the open garage, burying themselves deep in the walls. All the windows shattered. The roof caved in. A metal gutter burst through the back door. Within seconds, all that was left of the "pillar house" was a wrecked shell.

The school lay just ahead.

At Plainfield High School, Tim froze in the sudden darkness. Outside, the storm suddenly grew louder. *Much* louder. The wind was roaring like a freight train.

Coach Boe reached for the door handle, planning to stick his head outside to see what was happening. To his surprise, the door was stuck.

Then the fire alarm went off. "Get away from the door!" Coach DeSutter yelled.

Coach Boe jumped back, his face grim. The door wasn't stuck; the wind was keeping it closed! This wasn't an ordinary thunderstorm. This was something much, much worse.

In the dim light, Tim saw the look on his father's face. Coach Boe shouted, "Get down!" He pushed Tim down and covered him with his own body.

Squashed and scared, Tim heard Coach DeSutter yell, "Everybody get back out in the hall, *now!* Get down and cover your heads!" Several players ran out of the weight rooms, pulling on their football helmets. Tim thought he saw Kevin, but he didn't see Eric anywhere. Where was his brother? Down the hall, the door to the main gym burst open as the volleyball coach began to shove her players out. "Get out of here!" she yelled. "Hurry!" The football players quickly made room for the girls in the packed hallway.

When the last girl stepped out, the coach ran out behind her and slammed the door. Two seconds later, the main gym collapsed in a jumble of twisted steel and concrete.

Tim yelped in pain, clapping his hands to his ears. It felt like something was squeezing his eardrums. He tried plugging his ears with his fingers, but it didn't help. What was happening?

That was when he noticed a change in the howling wind. It was making an odd *swish-swish* sound now, like the sound of a drive-through car wash. And it was getting louder every second.

Thousands of feet above the school, a steel cargo container from a tractor-trailer flew in circles. Now, as the first winds tore into the school, the heavy container was dropped like a forgotten Matchbox truck. It slammed down, bursting through the window near the school's front entrance.

But the tornado wasn't finished with Plainfield High. It ripped its way across the low brick buildings, peeling back the roof and shattering the windows. Within seconds most of the school lay in ruins.

The tornado took only seconds to destroy the main gym. Now only the hallway and small gym were left standing—at least for the moment.

Awaiting the End

Adam DeSutter had been bunched up with the football players in the small gym when the lights went out. Not sure what was happening, the older boys had pulled Adam over against the wall and stationed themselves around him.

Now, as the roof above them began to shake, Ed took off his football helmet. "Here," he shouted over the roaring wind, shoving it down over Adam's head. "You keep this on!"

Adam nodded, his eyes wide in the darkness. The storm outside was louder than anything he'd ever heard. It sounded like a huge jet was passing right over their heads.

They all jumped when a jagged chunk of the roof above them disappeared. As rain and wind came thundering in, Adam began to scream. No matter how loud he yelled, he couldn't hear himself over the storm.

Out in the hallway, Tim was also screaming. The rumbling *swish-swish* of the wind was now so loud that he felt like his brain was going to explode. Dust was whipping through the air in front of him, and he suddenly felt cold. He shivered, goose bumps prickling his arms. Why was it getting so cold?

In the darkness and confusion, an overhead light crashed down, bringing part of the ceiling with it. The walls, the floor, everything was trembling. It felt like the whole building was going to fall apart.

The destructive tornado left the main gym in ruins. Underneath the rubble is the hallway where the nearly one hundred fifty students survived.

Tim held his head trying to block it all out. *Please help us,* he prayed, squeezing his eyes shut. *Please save us.*

The roaring and shaking seemed to go on forever. Then, suddenly, it was quiet again. Tim slowly looked up. Dozens of football players were crouching along the walls, hands over their helmets. The hall was covered with dust and chunks of ceiling tiles. Daylight was shining through the two weight room doors. That didn't make sense. The weight rooms didn't have windows. Where was the light coming from?

Tim uncurled himself. Coach Boe stood up. "Is everyone okay?" he shouted.

Beside them, Coach DeSutter also stood up. Down the hall, he could see Kevin jumping to his feet. He glanced around, looking for his younger son. "Adam!" he yelled in a panic. "Adam, where are you?"

Tim opened his mouth to say that Adam had been down in the small gym. Then Adam came running up the steps, wearing a football helmet three times his size.

"I'm right here, Dad!" he said. His father hugged him so tight that he almost couldn't breathe. Coach Boe found Eric and then went to help the volleyball coach comfort a girl who was crying. Several people had cuts or bruises, but nobody seemed to be badly hurt.

Coach DeSutter took a deep breath. "Okay, listen up!" he called. "Everybody line up so we can get a quick head count. We need to make sure we're not missing anybody."

They counted twice to make sure before the coaches led them out through the side door. One by one they stepped outside and then gasped. It was like walking out into an alien world.

"Man, can you believe this?" Eric said, squinting against the rain. It was slowed down now to a cold drizzle.

Adam looked back across the school—or what *used* to be the school. A thin trail of smoke rose from where the science lab used to be. Now it was only a heap of broken bricks and twisted metal. The main gym was flattened, and the two weight rooms were completely gone. The grass out front was covered with a tangle of fallen trees and broken glass.

"It's like a bomb hit us," Adam said in awe. "There's nothing left."

The only part still standing was the small hallway where they had taken refuge. A long line of football and volleyball players were still coming out, like ants marching out of an anthill. Somehow, they had chosen the one spot in the whole school where they would be safe.

Tim stared out at the football field. The heavy brick bleachers were gone, and all the metal light poles were twisted like pretzels. "I guess school won't be starting tomorrow," he said numbly. "There's no school left."

"Guess not," Coach Boe said. He looked like he was still in shock. "Thank God it happened today, instead of tomorrow. We'd have had over a thousand kids here."

Adam nudged Tim and pointed over to the parking lot. The cars had all been tumbled by the wind. Several had been smashed flat, including Billy's new Geo Storm. But now, compared with everything else, it didn't seem like a big deal.

"Okay," Coach DeSutter said when everybody was outside. "Let's head over to the Methodist church. Everybody stay together. If you see power lines down, stay away from them."

He led off across the front of the school, picking his way through all the rubble. The kids followed him single-file, like he was some kind of Pied Piper. They silently snaked their way down the street, hardly able to believe their eyes. It was like something out of an old war movie.

Several houses in Adam's neighborhood were flattened. Others just had big chunks taken out of them. Tim saw one house where a whole corner had been torn off leaving a frilly, pink bedroom sitting out in the open. The bed was still neatly made, and the loose papers on the dresser weren't even disturbed. The streets and yards were piled high with branches and broken pieces of houses. The few trees left standing were bare, like it was the middle of winter.

Adam stared when he spotted something long and white stuck in a tree branch. It was a pillar from his house!

"Dad!" he said, pointing. "That's our pillar!"

Coach DeSutter just nodded. There were too many other things to worry about right then.

They walked on. People started coming out into the streets to look around. Some of them were injured. In the distance, sirens began to wail. The air smelled like natural gas.

Lessons Learned the Hard Way

Ten minutes later they reached the Methodist church, but it was locked. They walked on to Central Elementary School. It was open. While the older kids used pay phones to call their parents, Adam and Tim stood on the front sidewalk, talking quietly.

"I wonder what would've happened to us if we'd stayed at your house," Tim said. "I bet we'd be dead right now."

"Maybe," Adam said. "It's weird that we saw it and didn't even know it was a tornado! It must've hit my house about five or ten minutes after we left."

"Pretty close."

"Yep." He looked over at Tim. "From now on, I'm going to listen to all the weather reports. I don't ever want to go through that again."

"Me too. And I'm not going to joke around anymore when they make us do those tornado drills at school. If I hear anything that even sounds like a tornado, I'll be out in the hall with my head down. Did you see what it did to all the windows? If you were standing next to one, you could get sucked right out or shot full of glass. I'm not taking any chances from now on."

Mrs. Boe burst out crying when she pulled up in front of the school and saw Tim. She ran over to hug him. "I'm so glad you're okay," she sobbed. "The news said a tornado had destroyed Plainfield High. I was so scared you'd all be hurt or dead!"

Tim didn't like to admit it, but after living through a tornado, it felt pretty good to be hugged by his mother. "I'm okay," he told her manfully. "We're all okay."

Adam felt the same way when his mom showed up. There were times when mothers, even hysterical, crying ones, were nice to have around. He hugged her hard. If Tim hadn't been standing there he might have cried too.

On television that night, the news said that the tornado had killed twenty-eight people and injured over three hundred fifty. At Plainfield High, a custodian and a teacher in another part of the building had been killed.

That night Adam had a hard time sleeping. Every time he closed his eyes he kept hearing the terrible roaring of the wind. After tossing and turning he finally laid back and stared up at the ceiling, thinking about things. It still didn't seem real that their house had been destroyed. His dad said it would take months to rebuild it. Until then, they would have to stay with relatives.

Adam sighed and buried his head in his pillow. Why, he wondered, had some people died while others lived? Was it because some people still had things they were supposed to do?

Maybe I'll be the first person to do something important, he thought sleepily. Like find a cure for AIDS or cancer. Maybe that's why I'm still alive.

Adam was shocked when he saw his house for the first time after the tornado. It was all bashed in and falling down. Doc's house and most of the other houses on their street looked just as bad. It made Adam want to cry or scream or kick something. Why did the stupid tornado have to tear up their neighborhood like that?

Mrs. DeSutter was upset that they had lost all the big trees in their yard, but Adam was cheered by the sight of the splintered stump of the crab apple tree.

"Can trees grow back from stumps?" he asked.

"No," Mrs. DeSutter said sadly.

Hiding a smile, Adam murmured, "Too bad." They might have lost their house, at least for a while, but at least he no longer had the job of picking up crab apples!

He was surprised when Doc walked across the street to join them. His perfect yard looked like a bomb crater now. Adam expected him to be furious about it, but he wasn't. He just smiled, absently jingling the change in his pockets.

"Some mess, huh?" he said to Adam. "It's a miracle more folks on our street weren't hurt or killed."

"Yeah," Adam said. He added awkwardly, "I'm sorry about all your flowers and stuff."

Doc shrugged. "I can always grow new ones. Something like this, it shows you what's really important. I'm glad none of you kids got hurt."

"I'm glad you're okay too," Adam said, surprised to find he really meant it. He was even more surprised to hear himself add, "Uh, if you need any help around your yard once we move back in, I'll be glad to help out."

Doc patted him on the shoulder. "That would be nice. Well, you take care!"

Adam felt a little dazed as he watched the older man walk back across the street. He couldn't wait to tell Tim about this. It looked like the tornado had made a *lot* of changes.

At least some of them weren't all bad!

Tim Boe (left) and Adam DeSutter in 1995
with *Real Kids Real Adventures* author,
Deborah Morris

Blanco River Rescue

The John Ruiz Story

Above: John Ruiz, age 13

The room was dark and quiet except for a faint snoring coming from two lumps huddled under the sheets. Those two lumps didn't move when the door slowly swung open and a dark, shadowy figure crept in.

One lump was thirteen-year-old John David Ruiz. The other was his best friend, Tony. On this hot summer night, Tony was spending the night at the Ruiz's house. They lived in the same neighborhood in San Antonio, Texas.

The shadowy figure paused in the doorway and then moved silently across the room toward the sleeping boys. Reaching the edge of the bed, it paused to pull out something hard that glinted in the moonlight.

Fingernail polish.

Diana Ruiz, John David's mom, grinned in the darkness, and then carefully lifted the sheet at the boys' feet. When their bare toes came in sight, she unscrewed the cap and dipped the small brush in the bright red polish.

"Payback time," she whispered, dabbing the polish onto their toenails. "You guys should know better by now than to give me a hard time."

John David sat up and yawned. He made a face as his morning breath drifted back at him. He hastily shut his mouth, trying to keep it in. He didn't want to gas poor Tony in his sleep.

Still half-asleep, he swung his legs around to the side of the bed and wiggled his toes, trying to work up enough energy to stand up. Then he saw his feet.

"Aargh!" he exclaimed, his eyes bugging out. He jumped out of bed, still staring down. Beside him, Tony woke up with a start.

"What's up?" he asked sleepily.

John David jerked the sheets off his friend's feet and pointed. Tony goggled when he saw his ten shiny red toenails. "What happened?" he sputtered.

"My *mom* happened," John David said, pointing down to his own feet. "She must've snuck in here last night while we were asleep. Remember how she said she'd get us back for teasing her?"

Tony nodded and broke into a grin. "I guess she got us, huh?"

"I guess so." John David shook his head ruefully. "We should've put socks on our hands and feet before bed or stacked up cans by the door. She did this to me once before. It was a school morning, and she hid the nail polish remover!"

Tony laughed. "What did you do?"

"Well, I scraped and scraped at it, but it wouldn't come off. She finally gave me the polish remover." Grinning, John David rubbed his hand across his short dark hair. "She's really bad!"

Mrs. Ruiz was waiting when they came out for breakfast. "Good morning, boys," she said sweetly. "Sleep well?"

John David gave her a skeptical look. "Where's the fingernail polish remover?"

Mrs. Ruiz frowned and tapped a finger to her cheek. "Hm, let's see. Fingernail polish remover. Now where did I see that?"

John David rolled his eyes. "See what I mean, Tony? She loves doing this to me! This is what I get for being a perfect teenager."

"Hey!" Mrs. Ruiz interrupted. "How many times do I have to tell you that you're not a teenager? You're just twelve plus one. I absolutely refuse to let my baby become a teenager."

"In another month I'll be fourteen. What're you gonna do then?"

Mrs. Ruiz smiled. "That's easy. Twelve plus two!"

Tony snickered. John David punched him.

"Hand over the polish remover, Mom. We want to go out, but we can't go anywhere looking like this!"

"Well," Mrs. Ruiz said, "I guess I'll give it to you just this once. But from now on you'd better watch out."

The boys quickly scrubbed off the polish and then took off on their bikes. The Ruizes lived in a one-story corner house with a big front yard. They had lived there for almost fourteen years, ever since the day John David was born.

Actually, he almost had been born *in* the house. Mrs. Ruiz was nine months pregnant when they first moved to San Antonio. While Mr. Ruiz stayed behind with their other two children to clean their old house, Mrs. Ruiz drove to San Antonio with her teenage brother. She went into labor on the way, scaring her little brother to death. By the time they reached the new house, John David was just minutes away from being born. Mrs. Ruiz got to the hospital just in time.

John David and Tony played basketball at the park for a while and then went to Tony's house to swim. Even in the water it was too hot to stay out in the sun for very long. Texas in the summer was about a zillion degrees. They finally went back to John David's house to relax.

Hanging Out at Home

Rudy Ruiz, John David's dad, had just come home from a business trip. Mr. Ruiz was a cheerful man with glasses and a shiny bald spot on top of his head. He kicked off his shoes and leaned back in his recliner.

"Hi, Dad!" John David said. "How was your trip?" He snatched up the TV remote and started flipping through the channels trying to find something good. If his father got to it first, he'd put it on Headline News or some other boring show.

"It went okay." Mr. Ruiz sounded tired, not at all like his usual self. John David looked at him sharply. His father's face looked a little gray.

"Hey, are you feeling all right?" Mr. Ruiz had almost died from a heart attack several years before. He still had a lot of chest pains, but he didn't like talking about it. He took nitro pills when the pain got too bad.

"I'm fine," Mr. Ruiz said, forcing a smile. "Just tired. I think I'll take a little nap."

John David looked over at Tony. They both knew Mr. Ruiz never took naps unless he was feeling bad. Tossing down the remote, John David went to find his mom. She was the only one who could drag it out of his dad when he was hurting.

They found Mrs. Ruiz down the hall trying to dust John David's room. She wasn't crazy about housework, and, since most of his furniture was covered with clothes and other junk, she was glad to stop. Like John David, she would rather be running around outside playing baseball than dusting knickknacks.

"What's up, guys?" she asked, straightening a small ceramic tennis shoe hung from a string on the wall. Across one side it said: "Yes, you can with Jesus!" John David had made it at Vacation Bible School the year before.

"It's Dad. I think his heart is hurting, but he won't say so. Can you go ask him what's wrong?"

Mrs. Ruiz tossed down her dust rag. "Yes. Thanks, honey." She hurried from the room, leaving John David relieved. The thought of his dad having another heart attack scared him. He and his older brother Trey kept their father's nitro pills stashed all around the house, just in case he ever needed them in a hurry. They had even stuffed some into the ashtray in his car.

By dinnertime, though, Mr. Ruiz seemed to be feeling better. When he wasn't sick, he liked to rush around and talk a lot.

"I saw this funny sign the other day," he said at dinner, stabbing a juicy piece of steak. "It had a pelican standing there with a frog in its mouth, and the frog had its hands around the pelican's throat. It said, 'Don't ever give up!'" He chuckled. "I made copies of it and passed it out to all my clients."

John David looked at Trey. The seventeen-year-old rolled his eyes. "Good one, Dad," he said.

"Hysterical," John David agreed.

Mrs. Ruiz hid a smile. Her husband's sense of humor had always been a little different from the rest of the family's. He liked jokes that had some deeper meaning. They liked to squirt each other with water guns or, better yet, crack raw eggs on each other's heads at Easter!

"I'm sure your clients all liked it," she said kindly.

"Don't you get it? It's inspiring!" he responded.

"Uh-huh," Trey said. Seeing his father reaching for the salt shaker, he moved fast to snatch it away. "Oh, no! You know you're not supposed to have salt."

Mr. Ruiz sighed. "But steak doesn't taste right without salt. *You* try it and see how you like it!"

"I don't have a bad heart," Trey said sternly. "Do I need to hide the salt shaker from you again?"

With a pained look, Mr. Ruiz took a bite of his unsalted steak and chewed it glumly. "It's better with salt," he grumbled. He joined in when the rest of them laughed, but he didn't like being nagged about his health. He soon changed the subject.

"I meant to tell you boys," he said, "I was talking to John today, and he says fishing's been good on the Blanco. They're catching a lot of smallmouth bass there now."

John Prodajko was an old friend of the family. Mrs. Ruiz had first met him years before when he played on her softball team. Since then he had become like one of the family. John David and Trey both called him "Uncle John."

"Can we go fishing there?" John David asked eagerly. "That sounds like fun."

Mr. Ruiz smiled. "I was thinking about it. I told John we might be able to go next Saturday. He's supposed to call back sometime next week."

After dinner, Mrs. Ruiz asked John David to vacuum the front room. Grumbling, he shoved the vacuum around a few times and then headed for the door.

Before he could get away, though, Mrs. Ruiz yelled, "John David, you come back here!" Sighing, he turned and trudged back inside. His mom was standing in the front room, tapping her foot. She pointed down to the carpet. "Do you call this vacuumed?"

John David studied the ceiling and then the wall behind her head. "Yes," he told the wall firmly, "I do."

"Well, I don't. There's still stuff all over the carpet. What did you do, just wiggle the vacuum around a few times and call it good?"

"Uh, not exactly." Come to think of it, that was exactly what he'd done. But it wouldn't do any good to admit that now!

"Well, here's what I want you to do since you've already *vacuumed.*" Mrs. Ruiz sighed. She paused to give him a hard look. "I guess you can just crawl around and pick up every last little bit of junk that's left on the floor."

"Aw, Mom! Can't it wait until later?"

"Nope. Now." She pointed down and added threateningly, "And I'm going to check it, so you'd better do a good job this time."

Sighing, John David dropped to his hands and knees. His mother was too hard on him. His dad would have just said, "Do it better next time, okay?" Or better yet, he would have grabbed the vacuum and said, "Here, let me show you how to do it right!" By the time he finished, it would have been perfect. John David liked his dad's approach a lot better than his mom's.

He liked his dad's rules better too. Mr. Ruiz usually let him try stuff, like racing his bike down steep hills. If he ended up with scraped knees or a bloody nose, that was his own problem. Mrs. Ruiz always thought something horrible was going to happen. She wouldn't even let him ride to the park at night to play basketball with his friends. She acted like monsters were waiting to grab him.

He wedged his head under the edge of the couch and peered around, hoping a stray five-dollar bill might be hiding there. But the only thing stuffed under there was an old newspaper. It just wasn't his day! As he crawled back and forth, picking up torn paper and tiny hair wads, he suddenly grinned. This was kind of like being a carpet catfish. Catfish cruised the river bottoms sucking up junk; he cruised the carpet picking up hair wads.

Thinking of catfish reminded him of the fishing trip they talked about at dinner. He hoped it would work out. It would be fun to go fishing on the Blanco River.

With that happy thought he zoomed over, catfish-like, to scoop up another carpet-fuzz wad.

Up before Dawn

It was still dark outside when a voice jolted John David out of a confusing dream—something about baseball and Tony and spaghetti and turtles.

"Time to get up," Mr. Ruiz said again from the doorway. "We've got fishing to do!"

John David squinted at the clock and groaned. Five o'clock in the morning! Getting up that early on a Saturday, even to go fishing, was hard. He rolled out of bed and staggered over to his dresser, trying to pick out clothes without opening his eyes. Uncle John was supposed to be there at nine. Before he got there, they needed to load their inflatable boat and all their fishing gear in the truck.

Mr. Ruiz was in the kitchen sipping a cup of coffee when John David stumbled in a few minutes later. "Morning," John David grunted.

"Morning, son," Mr. Ruiz said brightly. He was always disgustingly cheerful in the mornings. "Ready to catch some fish?"

"Right now I'm ready to go back to bed. Once I wake up I might be ready to catch fish."

"Good!" Mr. Ruiz beamed. "Grab some breakfast and come out back. We need to load the boat into Trey's truck."

That woke up John David. His dad wasn't supposed to lift or strain because of his heart. But if somebody else wasn't there to help, he probably would try to do it all himself.

"I'll be right out," John David said. "Where's Trey?" His brother wasn't going fishing with them, but he had volunteered to drive the boat there in his truck.

Once it was inflated, it wouldn't fit into the back of their car. They planned to stop at a gas station on the way to have it blown up.

"I think he's already out back."

John David wolfed down some cereal and then headed for the garage. He found his dad pulling handfuls of line off his favorite fishing reel. A huge, tangled clump of it was lying on the floor.

"My line's gotten old and brittle," Mr. Ruiz explained. "We'll have to stop at Wal-Mart on the way and pick up some new line and maybe a few new lures."

John David nodded. "Want Trey and me to load the boat in his truck now?" Even though it was an inflatable, the four-man fishing raft was large and heavy. They kept it rolled up out in the shed.

Mr. Ruiz put down his fishing rod. "Trey and I will take care of it. Why don't you go dig up some fishing worms?"

John David followed his dad outside, planning to keep an eye on him. He knew his dad would be too stubborn to stop if the boat got too heavy for him. If it looked like he was straining, John David planned to run in to help. But Trey took care of the problem by taking most of the weight himself. Once the boat was safely in the truck, John David wandered off to hunt worms.

They had some black, wormy dirt along one side of their house. John David squatted down and used a stick to stir the dirt around, watching for wiggling. Spotting a long, fat worm, he grabbed it and pulled. It slid out of the dirt, its body curling into pretzel shapes. He admired it for a moment before dropping it into his bucket. Soon the bottom was a tangle of wiggling worms.

Good thing worms can't scream, he thought in amusement. None of them looked too happy about being dragged out of the ground, but if they knew where they were going they would probably be screaming their little heads off.

"You guys are bait," he said cheerfully. "Live with it!"

"Who're you talking to?"

John David jumped and turned around. His brother was standing behind him grinning.

"I was just telling the worms to save their energy," John David replied with dignity. "I want them to be in good shape so I can catch a lot of bass."

"How many you got?"

John David tipped the bucket so his brother could see.

"Looks good," Trey said. "So when is Uncle John supposed to be here?"

"Around nine. What time is it now?"

"Ten after. Are you ready?"

John stood up and brushed the worm dirt off his knees. "Pretty much. But before we go, I want to check Dad's tackle box to make sure his nitro pills are still in there."

"They are. I already looked." They smiled at each other in quick understanding. They planned to keep their dad alive and well to a ripe old age, whether he liked it or not.

Of course, being brothers, they didn't always get along that well. In fact, it had only been a few weeks since their last big fight.

A "Tortured" Past

It started one day when Trey's friend Louis came over. John David shoved the two older boys, trying to pick a playful fight. He kept it up until they both got mad and grabbed him. When Trey asked Louis what they should do with him, they agreed torture might be nice.

John David laughed as Trey and Louis tied his feet together and then tied his hands to two doorknobs. But once he realized he couldn't get away, he got mad. "You better untie me, or I'll tell Mom!" he threatened. "C'mon, Trey!"

His brother only smiled. "I think a little Chinese water torture might be fun, don't you, Louis? We could videotape the whole thing."

Louis grinned. "Great idea! Let's get the camera."

As they headed down the hall, John David sputtered, "Hey! Come back here, you guys! This isn't funny!"

Soon the older boys reappeared with a video camera, an ice cube, and some fishing line. Trey used the fishing line to tie the ice cube over John David's head, adjusting it carefully so it would drip on him as it melted. Meanwhile, Louis videotaped every moment. They left John David tied up, kicking and squirming, for a few minutes and then came back and untied him.

When Mrs. Ruiz came home John David complained to her about being tortured. She rolled her eyes.

"Don't exaggerate," she said. "You know your brother wouldn't torture you." She wasn't convinced until John David showed her the videotape.

But the effect wasn't exactly what he had hoped for. As Mrs. Ruiz watched the video of him squirming around with the ice cube dripping on him, she started giggling. Even John David had to admit that he had looked pretty funny.

Mrs. Ruiz wiped her eyes and said weakly, "Trey, I don't want you torturing your little brother any more. It isn't very nice, even if you're playing around."

Trey shot John David a triumphant grin. It was nice to have a mom with a warped sense of humor. "Okay, Mom. But can I lock him in the closet if he gives me too much trouble?"

Mrs. Ruiz gave him a stern look. "No. Absolutely not. Unless," she added, her lips twitching again mischievously, "I'm there to watch."

"Mo-om!" John David protested. Okay, so the "torture" hadn't been so bad. Still, he wanted Trey to get in *some* trouble.

"Calm down, I'm just kidding." She added seriously, "Really, Trey, you're old enough to know that you can hurt people by acting silly. What if the house had caught on fire? What if your brother had needed to get to medicine really fast? What if he got so upset he couldn't breathe? What if...."

"All right, Mom, I get the picture!" Trey said hastily. "I'll never torture him again, no matter how much he deserves it. Which is," he muttered darkly, "a lot."

Trey apologized, and before long the two brothers were laughing together about the whole "torture" incident. John David saved the videotape as a souvenir.

Off to the Blanco

Waiting to leave on the fishing trip, John David was getting impatient. Where was Uncle John? At nine-thirty, he finally wandered back into the house. He found his mom in her bedroom, still in her robe.

"Uncle John is really late," he complained. "Has he called or anything?"

"No, but I'm sure he'll show up soon." Mrs. Ruiz patted him on the arm. "Listen, take care of your dad for me while you're out, okay? I always worry about him doing too much."

"Don't worry, Mom. I'll watch out for him."

An hour later, Uncle John finally showed up. An Army sergeant, he was tall and skinny with short blond hair. "Sorry I'm so late," he said, jumping out of his car. "Is everybody else ready?"

"Yep," Mr. Ruiz said. "We've already got everything loaded. Trey's bringing the boat in his truck."

They threw Uncle John's gear into the back of the car and took off. John David relaxed in the back seat, planning to nap during the long, boring drive. But when they pulled into Wal-Mart, his father sent him in to buy the fishing line and lures they needed.

The fishing aisle at Wal-Mart had always been one of his favorite spots. He grabbed a spool of fishing line and went to look at lures. He was supposed to buy six, but it was hard to decide between them. He ended up buying almost a dozen, all different colors and sizes.

When he returned to the car, Mr. Ruiz raised an eyebrow. "Went a little lure-crazy, didn't you? I thought I said *six*."

"I figured we could use some extras," John David said. He looked to his uncle for support. "Besides, they were cheap."

Uncle John nodded. "I've always said you can never have too many lures. Probably should've bought *two* dozen."

"Right!" John David agreed.

Mr. Ruiz looked from his friend to his son and then chuckled. "I know when I'm beaten. I guess I should just be glad you didn't buy *three* dozen!" He put the car in reverse. "Can you do me a favor and put that new line on my reel, son? It'll save time later."

"Sure." John David reached back to grab his dad's fishing rod and then propped it between his knees. He had never put on new line by himself, but it didn't look hard. You just started the line and cranked it in until the fishing reel was full.

But after reeling for a long time, John David frowned. Was that enough line? Too much? Just enough? He couldn't tell. He turned the handle a few more times just to be safe and then cut the line. He hoped he had done it right.

Thirty minutes later they stopped at a gas station to inflate the boat. It quickly puffed up into a big, sturdy boat. It was white and orange on top and dark red on the bottom. The boat could hold four or five people.

By the time they reached the Blanco River, it was almost four o'clock. Trey helped Uncle John slide the boat off the truck and carry it down to the water.

"Well, I hope you guys have a good time," Trey said as he got back into his truck. "Catch lots of fish!" He gave John David a long look and then nodded toward their father. The younger boy understood.

It was a look that said, "Take care of Dad."

After they unloaded the rest of the fishing gear, Mr. Ruiz suddenly slapped his forehead. "I forgot the mounting rods! I can't believe I did that. How are we going to hook up the motor?"

The motor usually hooked on to metal rods that fit across the back of the boat. But Mr. Ruiz soon came up with another idea. By stringing a yellow tow rope through some metal rings at the back of the boat, he made a kind of "rope rod" to hold the motor. It worked great!

"Okay," he said happily, "time for some serious fishing!"

John David stepped carefully into the small boat and sat down at the very front. Uncle John sat in the middle, and Mr. Ruiz sat back by the motor. Soon they were heading out toward the middle of the river.

Once they were away from the shore, John David tied a bright orange lure onto his line and cast it out. His father and Uncle John did the same.

Mr. Ruiz's lure only went a little way before jerking to a stop and plunking straight down into the water. He looked at his reel and frowned. "Son, how much line did you put on my reel? There's not even enough for me to cast!"

"I put it on until it looked full. I wasn't really sure how to do it. I'd never done it by myself before."

Mr. Ruiz sighed. "I guess I'm not going to be catching much today, unless the fish swim right up to the boat. There isn't enough line left to fill the reel."

John David hung his head. "Sorry, Dad. You want to trade rods with me?"

Mr. Ruiz shook his head. He never stayed upset for long. "Don't worry about it. It's my own fault for not showing you how to do it before I asked you." He cast his short line out again, laughing this time when it stopped in midair.

They fished quietly for a while, casting in different directions so they wouldn't get their lines tangled. No one caught anything. They finally switched lures and moved down the river trying to find a better spot.

But no matter where they tried, they still didn't get a nibble. After several fishless hours Mr. Ruiz complained, "I thought you said it was good fishing here, John! Where are all the bass you promised?"

"Not where *we* are, that's for sure," Uncle John said. "Let's keep moving. They've got to be hiding here somewhere."

Just ahead was a low-water crossing where a road stretched across the river. When the water was low enough, the road stuck up a few inches above like a flat bridge. A pipe underneath let the river flow through to the other side.

But when the river was high, like this time, water covered the top of the road. Mr. Ruiz stopped the motor and let the boat drift closer.

"Get ready," he said. "We're going to have to get out and carry the boat across."

The boat scraped onto the edge of the road. John David hopped out. The water over the road was ankle-deep, tumbling along with the current. He grabbed one side of the boat and lifted.

"Be careful, Dad," he cautioned when his father bent to lift the other side. "Don't strain."

Mr. Ruiz gave him an irritated look. "I think I can handle this. You just worry about keeping your end up."

They dragged the boat across and dropped it back in the water on the other side. They slowly fished their way downstream dragging the boat over several more low-water crossings.

But by seven-thirty that evening, they were all fed up. They had tried all their favorite lures and even all the new ones John David had bought. They hadn't caught even one puny, old fish.

John David finally decided to try one of his worms. He picked a big, fat juicy one and poked it onto his hook. It was a fighter and lashed back and forth. It would make good bait. He cast it out, not really expecting to catch anything.

It wasn't long, though, before he felt a huge tug on his line. The tip of his rod bent down, following his line as it curved away through the water.

"I've got one!" he yelled. "I've got a fish!" He reeled as fast as he could, afraid it would get away.

Mr. Ruiz and Uncle John both cheered him on. When he pulled the flapping fish up from the water, Uncle John exclaimed, "It's a catfish! Swing it over here so I can grab your line!"

Uncle John was leaning out, reaching for the line, when the boat suddenly tilted. They had all been so busy watching the catfish that they hadn't noticed how quickly the next crossing was coming up. This one was a low concrete bridge. In front of it, water was being sucked down into a small, underwater drain, forming a whirlpool. They had drifted right into it.

Sucked into Disaster

The next few seconds were a blur. John David's fishing rod flew out of his hands and landed in the water. He was tossed sideways away from the boat. The next thing he knew, he landed with a splash on top of the bridge.

Stunned, he scrambled to his feet. The lid to their ice chest floated past him and was swept over the bridge by the rushing current. What had happened?

"Son, grab hold of me!" Mr. Ruiz's desperate cry snapped the thirteen-year-old out of his confusion. He looked down to see his father clinging to the side of the bridge, his face gray with shock. The inflatable boat was curled around behind him, pinning him against the concrete. His legs, out of sight under the bridge, were caught in the roaring whirlpool. As the water dragged him down, his fingers were slipping down the side of the bridge. He was only seconds from being sucked under. In a panic, John David dropped to his knees and grabbed his father's T-shirt. When he tried to pull him up, Mr. Ruiz cried out in pain.

"Don't pull!" he said. "My legs are stuck!"

John David looked around wildly. Spotting his uncle flailing in the water a few feet away, he yelled, "Uncle John! Come help my dad!"

But Uncle John was having trouble of his own. He was also caught in the current. He was pulling himself inch by inch along the bridge, fighting to break free. One slip and he would be gone.

"I'm trying!" Uncle John shouted. "Just hang on!"

John David's arms were already feeling the strain of holding his father's weight. The current was shoving the heavy boat against Mr. Ruiz's back, making it even harder to hold on to him. The whirlpool kept trying to suck him under. "Are you okay, Dad?" he asked anxiously.

Mr. Ruiz's face was strained. "Something's hurting my back." A big tackle box was caught between his back and the boat. John David pulled it out and tossed it up onto the bridge. "Is that better?"

"Yes," Mr. Ruiz answered.

The teenager could tell his father was getting weak. He was barely hanging on. "Hurry, Uncle John!" he pleaded. He held on grimly, ignoring the shooting pains in his arms and shoulders.

"Something's wrapped around my leg," Mr. Ruiz said hoarsely. "It's hurting really bad."

"Just hang on. You'll be okay." John David knew if his dad said something hurt bad, it was *really* bad. What if he was having another heart attack? He held on grimly, pleading with Uncle John to hurry. His arms were now trembling with the strain.

Then, to his horror, he felt his father slipping from his hands. Mr. Ruiz slid down until the rushing water came up almost to his chin. "Dad!" John David gasped. He grabbed him under the arms, trying to get a better hold. Mr. Ruiz groaned, hardly seeming to notice what had happened.

I can't do this, John David thought in despair. I can't hold him!

Yes, you can with Jesus!

The words on the little shoe he'd made in Vacation Bible School came back to him unexpectedly. Looking up, he screamed, "Jesus, help me! Please don't let him die!"

Mr. Ruiz closed his eyes. "Let's pray together for strength, son," he gasped. "I can't stand this much longer."

John David leaned down to press his forehead to his father's. All he could think was, *Please help my dad. Please don't let him die.* He thought it as hard as he could, over and over, hoping God might hear. He wasn't sure how prayer and all that stuff worked.

Then, to his relief, he felt his uncle's strong arms reaching down beside him. Dripping and out of breath, Uncle John said, "I've got him."

But when they tried to pull him up, Mr. Ruiz once again screamed with pain. "My leg! Stop pulling!"

"Dad, are you okay? How's your heart?"

Mr. Ruiz looked sick, like he was going to faint. He ignored the question about his heart. "There's something wrapped around my leg. It feels like it's cutting it in half."

Just then a small truck drove up the gravel road beside the river. It skidded to a stop at the edge of the bridge. There were three girls inside. They stared out at the bridge.

Uncle John jumped up and waved frantically. "Do you have a phone?"

John David was afraid the girls might ignore them and drive off. "We need help!" he yelled. *"Go get help!"*

The girl in the driver's seat stuck her head out the window. "I'm on my way!" she yelled to them. She pulled out onto the water-covered bridge, driving slowly to keep from splashing as she passed them. When she got to the other side, she sped off with a spurt of gravel.

Mr. Ruiz groaned. Uncle John tapped John David on the shoulder. "I'll hold him again. Go get a knife out of the tackle box. Maybe we can cut him loose from whatever's wrapped around his leg."

All John David could find in the tackle box was an old fishing knife. He touched the blade doubtfully. It was dull, but it was all they had. It would have to do.

Lying flat on his stomach, he slid his hand down his father's leg. His fingers brushed a thin, knotted strand.

"I found something!" he said. "I think it's a rope."

"Hurry," Mr. Ruiz said. His eyes were glazed with pain. "Please hurry."

John David attacked the rope, hacking at it with the dull knife. It took several minutes, but it finally parted. "Got it!" he whooped, holding up a dripping white strand.

But when he tried to lift his father again, something was still holding him down. "It must be the yellow tow rope," Mr. Ruiz said weakly. "I can still feel it around my leg. It's attached to the boat."

John David looked at the knife. "Why don't I just pop the boat? Then maybe we could pull the whole thing up with you."

"I'm afraid it would drag me down. The boat's helping me stay afloat."

John David flung himself back down again. He reached back under the bridge, feeling along his father's leg. His heart sank when his fingertips brushed another thicker rope. It *was* the tow rope. It would take forever to cut.

But there was no other choice. He slipped the dull blade under the rope and started sawing at it. Mr. Ruiz moaned.

"It won't be much longer," John David said. "It's gonna be okay."

He had cut a small groove in the rope when it suddenly slipped from his fingers. He grabbed at it, but it was too late. He couldn't find the cut spot again. He would have to start all over.

"Let's trade places," Uncle John suggested. John David handed him the knife and moved over to hold his father. By now, Mr. Ruiz was almost crazy with pain.

"Just let me go," he begged. "My leg hurts too bad. I can't take this anymore!"

"No! I'm not letting go!" Biting his lip, the teenager determined to hang on no matter what. The thought of life without his father made him feel cold inside. He couldn't let him die.

Trying to Hold On

Please, he began to pray again. *Please don't let this happen.* It was easier to pray this time. He just hoped it would help.

Uncle John was still sawing at the rope when the truck came back. The girl had brought a man back with her. They drove onto the bridge and jumped out.

"Can you help my dad?" John David shouted.

The man was already bending down to take off his shoes. "I don't know, but I'll try!" He quickly threw his shoes aside. "My name's Rex. I live right down the road. We called 911 before we left."

John David explained that his father's leg was tangled in a rope. Rex nodded. "If you'll let me use your knife, I'll go down there and try to cut it off him," he offered.

Alarmed, Uncle John said, "You can't get in the water! I almost didn't make it out. The whirlpool's really strong."

Rex stared down at the foaming water and then pointed. "See the little concrete wall down there? If I stand behind that, away from the whirlpool, I should be safe. I think I can do it."

John David squinted down at the water. Sure enough, two low walls angled out from the bridge, funneling the whirlpool between them. Why hadn't they seen that before?

Mr. Ruiz was in agony. "My leg's getting cut off!"

he gasped. "Just let me go. I'll probably just get sucked under the bridge and come out on the other side." His face twisted with pain. "Please, son, let me go!"

John David shook his head. "You might get stuck inside the pipe. You're going to be okay, Dad. Just hold on a few minutes longer."

Rex slipped into the water and made his way over to the small wall. Bracing his knees against it, he leaned over it as far as he could. When he found the rope cutting into Mr. Ruiz's leg, he slipped the knife under it.

Mr. Ruiz drew in his breath. John David held him tighter. "It's all right, Dad. Everything's going to be okay."

Rex sawed at the rope for a few minutes with the dull blade. Finally, he tossed it aside and pulled out a pocket knife. "This is old, but it's sharp," he said. "I think it'll cut better." Sure enough, he soon sliced through the last strand of rope. Mr. Ruiz was free!

John David pulled and Rex pushed to get Mr. Ruiz up onto the bridge. The moment they lifted him from the water, the boat was sucked down into the whirlpool. John David threw his arms around his father.

"You made it!" he cried. "You're gonna be all right, Dad."

Mr. Ruiz nodded, his face twisted with pain as he rubbed his leg. John David glanced over at the other side of the bridge to see if the boat had ever come out. It hadn't. He shivered. That's what would have happened to his father if he had let him go!

An ambulance soon pulled up, sirens screaming. John David ran to meet the EMTs (emergency medical technicians).

"Listen, my dad's got heart problems," he told a short woman with dark hair. "You've got to watch him."

"Okay, thanks." Grabbing a small box of medical supplies, she motioned for the others to follow. John David trotted along as they started out across the bridge. He wanted to make sure they all knew about his dad's heart. He tapped the arm of another EMT, a woman with long hair.

"My dad might need a nitro pill," he said. "He has a really bad heart. He almost died a couple years ago. You have to watch him."

"Okay," the woman said. "We'll take care of him. Don't worry."

As they bent over his father, John David stood nearby. Mr. Ruiz's left leg was purple, puffy, and striped with red rope marks. Suddenly, a loud *boom!* echoed through the air. The inflatable boat, battered almost to pieces, had finally come shooting out of the underwater drain pipe.

John David looked at his father, a lump in his throat. *Thank You,* he thought silently. *Thank You for helping me hold on to him.*

Mr. Ruiz got to go home later that night. His leg was bruised and swollen, and it would hurt for a long time. Other than that he was all right.

John David didn't really relax until he saw his dad settled into bed that night. For the first time since the accident, he felt like his job was done. Feeling tired and numb, he collapsed on the couch. A few minutes later, his mother came over and sat next to him.

"Your father tells me if it wasn't for you, he'd have died today," she said softly.

"All I did was hold on to him, Mom. I promised you this morning I'd take care of him, and I did."

"You sure did." Mrs. Ruiz smiled, her eyes filled with tears. "I guess this means I have to finally admit that you're growing up, doesn't it? You acted like a man today, not a twelve-plus-one. I'm proud to have a *teenager* like you."

John David and his father, safe
after their nearly fatal boat accident

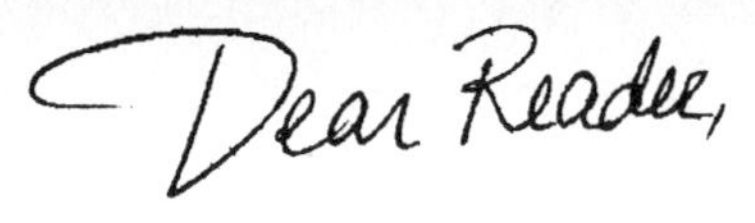

Have you heard or read about someone who should be a "Real Kid"?

Here's what it takes to be a "Real Kids" story:

1. It has to be TRUE. All the stories in *Real Kids Real Adventures* are told just as they happened. I can't use made-up stories, no matter how exciting they are.

2. It has to INVOLVE KIDS between the ages of 8 and 17. Younger kids and adults can be involved, but the main characters must be kids and teens.

3. It has to be DRAMATIC. *Real Kids Real Adventures* is about kids who are heroes or survivors, not about things like diseases or child abuse.

4. It has to have happened IN THE LAST THREE YEARS. It can take a year (or more) for a book to be published or a TV episode to be filmed. We'd like the kids to still be kids when their stories come out!

5. It has to have a HAPPY ENDING!

If you find a story, send me a newspaper clipping or other information to help me track it down. If I'm able to use it (and if you are the first one to tell me about that particular story) I'll print your name in the book and send you a free autographed copy when it comes out.

Let me know what you think of this volume of *Real Kids Real Adventures*. You can write to me at: P.O. Box 461572, Garland, TX 75046-1572, or email me at deb@realkids.com.

Deborah Morris